"I can wait," he said.

"But why should you wait?" she asked slowly, feeling a chill in her stomach.

"Because you asked me to come here tonight."

"I asked you?" she repeated, staring at him.

"Sure. Don't you remember when we met on the sidewalk the other night you smiled at me? I knew you meant for me to come and see you."

"See me?" she said, unable to take her eyes away from his own piercing ones.

He quickly put his hand under her skirt and squeezed the warm flesh of her thighs. "I want to see you with nothing on."

She sat perfectly still while he rolled back the hem of her skirt and admired her thighs.

She knew who he was then and knew that any one gesture that frightened him would mean her death.

PROWLER IN THE NIGHT

JACK MATCHA

FAWCETT PUBLICATIONS, INC.
FAWCETT BLDG., FAWCETT PLACE, GREENWICH, CONN.

to Ruth Breakstone—with love

1

THE TALL BLONDE GIRL lay spread-eagled in the sun, her burnished legs spanning the white terry-cloth robe on the lawn. It was early in the afternoon. The small fence around the grass and the tree of Heaven at one end assured the sun worshiper privacy. She let the top of her bathing suit down, reveling in the luxurious warmth of the sun's rays. Then she lay back, stretching out her legs boldly and offering her round breasts to the sun, sure that only a low-flying plane could violate the delicious sense of being alone on the top of a hill overlooking Hollywood.

In her lassitude and mesmerized state, she did not hear the tiny squeak of the fence gate as it swung inward. She did not hear the slight footsteps of the intruder who stopped a dozen feet away and stared at her naked body. Something must have warned her, though he made no sound. Perhaps it was some small sense of guilt at offering herself nakedly to the sun, even in her isolated surroundings. Perhaps she expected a visitor at just that moment and remembered too late and wondered if he were coming. Perhaps the power of his eyes, as he continued to stare at her, disturbed and awakened her.

In any case, she opened her eyes and saw the man looking down at her. A terrible premonition seized her and formed a scream in her throat. It was emasculated by her fear. She heard nothing: he continued to stare at her, smiling now and watching her terror. For a few seconds the watcher and the watched remained transfixed, unable to change their positions, as if they were caught in a block of marble. Then the girl flushed and rose quickly and ran toward the house.

This time the scream came, loud and sharp. But in the hot afternoon sun, on the lawn on the steep hill, it seemed pathetically lost. The nearest house seemed to be an eternity away down the slope. A woman dozing on a porch glider in that house thought she heard a scream, but could not be sure.

The girl never reached the house. Halfway to the door, she was brought down by a flying tackle. The man's hand stifled her screams while he held her body down with his body. The touch of her flesh seemed to startle him and he took his hand away from her mouth. He looked at her and drew back a little as if astounded by what he had done. He began to rise and back away. If she had remained silent, he might have fled. But suddenly she began to scream again, this time loudly. He seized her throat and strangled her slowly while her distended eyes stared at him petrified with fear.

Just before the life went out of her forever a tiny flicker of recognition appeared in her eyes. The intruder kept his hands around her throat long after she was dead. He seemed unable to move. Only when he heard the sound of an automobile's tires moving along the road twenty yards away, did he get up. He looked at what he had done. Then he stooped to kiss the dead lips and covered the body tenderly with the terry-cloth robe. He left silently, picking up his heavy bundle wrapped in coarse paper.

The woman in the house below heard the second scream and became frightened. She called the police immediately and shut her windows, for she remembered suddenly that a prowler or a sex criminal had attacked women in the area a few days earlier. When the patrol car from the Hollywood precinct arrived she was so cowed by terror that she was afraid to let them in.

Half an hour later, one of the two policemen, a short, plump man with spaniel-like brown eyes and little hair, spoke wearily into the telephone of the murdered woman.

"Jenkins? Lieutenant Goldberg. Yeah. Up in Laurel Canyon. We found a dead woman. A girl named Carol Forsythe. Seems to have been an actress. Strangled. Don't know yet whether she was raped. Send Doc up when you can and the photographer. And for Christ sake try to keep the goddamned reporters away for at least an hour, so we can look around. Yeah, I know this is the third one in this neighborhood. I know. I know. What do you want me to do? I ain't got radar in my head. I had rocks in my head when I left Brooklyn. They don't go strangling blondes taking sunbaths there. Of course they don't sunbathe in the nude either. All right, I'll give you the rest later. You got the address."

He hung up and looked wearily at the body under the terry-cloth robe. "I can just see the headline tonight," he said to the uniformed policeman. He shook his head. "I had rocks in my head. I had to come to California."

The other detective chuckled and answered as if on cue. He was a tall, rawboned, Irish-faced man with a rubber tire that was getting too big around his middle. "So why don't you go on back? Who's keeping you here? I'm sick of hearing you New Yorkers bitch about this place."

Lieutenant Goldberg did not even bother to look up from the desk where he was going through the girl's letters. "Why don't I go back, he asks. Don't ask me, ask my wife. Like all women—she thinks because a place has sunshine, it's heaven. What the hell have you got here? A smog so stinking you can't drive without thinking your god-damned eyes are going to fall out. And sun, sun, sun all day—every god-damned day of the year. You ever realize how nice it is to get one cloudy day once in a while? Just one lousy day when the sun doesn't shine. Do you, Farley?"

"I like the sun," Farley said righteously.

It was their favorite topic and they fell into it automatically whenever they went out together. Farley was one of the few native Californians Goldberg had met—a man who had spent all thirty-eight years of his life in California, except for three during the war. He felt it his duty to defend his home state against all comers, Easterners in particular. When Lieutenant Goldberg had joined the Los Angeles Police after ten years on the New York force, he and Farley had begun a good-natured feud almost the day they met.

They checked all the papers and photographs in the girl's desk and went through her drawers and valises.

"Nothing," Goldberg said finally. "This bastard—if it's the same guy—is a shrewd character. How he walks into these places and manages to get these dames without exciting any attention, God only knows."

"Maybe he's a traveling salesman and dates them up," Farley said laughing.

"Oh, brother, are you funny," Lieutenant Goldberg replied.

He returned to the girl's body and examined it carefully. He studied the red marks on the girl's legs where the killer had dug with his sharp fingernails, the bruises on her torso.

9

"Was she raped?" Farley asked.

"No, he'd have ripped her suit off and spread her legs. I think he got scared when she tried to scream or fight him off and choked her." He kneeled by the body. A few inches away he found a cigarette stub with lipstick on it, some hairpins and some pieces of torn cellophane.

Goldberg stared at the dead girl's pale breasts, so white against the olive-tinted flesh of her thighs. "I'd like to cover her up, but I guess I'd better wait till the photographer gets here." He removed a thick cigar from his lapel pocket and angrily ripped at the cellophane wrapper. "Jesus how I'd like to get my hands around that bastard's windpipe. If there's anything that really disgusts me it's a sex criminal. And these nuts infest this town. Peepers, perverts, every slob you can name."

He saw Farley's face harden and look away a moment. Goldberg felt like kicking himself. He had forgotten the Irishman's nephew who had been discharged from the Army during the Korean War as a psychoneurotic. The boy, whose parents were dead, lived alone with his uncle. Farley had been sending him to a series of psychiatrists for years.

"I'm sorry, Jim," Goldberg said. "I didn't mean your nephew. I know they picked him up in an alley, but he wasn't peeping. There's nothing wrong with the kid. He just has to readjust."

"That's okay, Abe," Farley said. "I was just thinking how long the boy's been seeing these mental experts and he's still unable to work."

Goldberg nodded understandingly. "You're like the Rock of Gibraltar, you stubborn Irishman. You could have made lieutenant by now, if you spent more time on your job and less nursing that kid. To say nothing of that correspondence school law course. Why the hell don't you get married?"

"I can't afford it after paying the psychiatrist," Farley said, grinning. He pointed to the body. "You really think it's the same prowler who attacked the woman yesterday?"

Goldberg nodded. "The same guy. The only thing that bothers me is that the woman says she was raped. The trouble is that this particular boy never would have raped her.

"He didn't rape this girl. And he didn't rape the woman in Gardenia either. Apparently he likes to strip them and maul them. See the dirt on the girl's breasts and notice the finger marks on her thighs? Why would he rape this other girl yesterday?"

Farley looked thoughtful. "I have an idea she may not

have been raped. That's what she told us she thought happened—but actually she was unconscious. Let me call the girl's doctor."

Goldberg nodded. When Farley had gone inside, he looked around the grounds again and then down at the winding street that led to Hollywood Boulevard. Somewhere in that tangle of streets was a psychotic killer who stalked women like a hunter.

The police photographer's arrival interrupted his thoughts. The man took several pictures of the body from every angle, working silently, efficiently. When he was finished he said, "Seems to like 'em all young. Got good taste anyway." Then he left.

Farley came out a moment later. "Her doctor says there was no penetration. Finger marks on her breasts and thighs and some slight bruises around the pubic area. But he didn't try to have intercourse."

"It's our man, then," Goldberg said quietly. "And the only reason he didn't kill her was he heard someone coming down the stairs. Two murders and one near-murder in one week. And God only knows where the bastard goes next. So far we haven't a clue.

"From what I can put together," Goldberg went on, "the guy is obsessed with sex, but he either hates it or fears it. He goes after girls below thirty, he strips them, feels them up, bites them, maybe even wrestles with them. But he never tries to rape them. Afteward he probably kills them because he's scared they'll give him away. Or maybe he works himself up to a sexual frenzy that ends with strangulation. My guess though is he only kills them when they make a move that scares him.

"He's probably a very innocent-looking guy—the type normally seen around these neighborhoods," Goldberg said. "None of the known skid-row bums or sex nuts could have done this. We know that. It's somebody not on our list: the guy may never even have been picked up before."

Goldberg scowled at Farley.

"The Commissioner's on my neck now. And the damned papers are running editorials about the prowler scare every day. Jesus, wouldn't I love to be some egghead sitting on my can in an air-conditioned news office, writing about the horrible inefficiency of the police. Christ if we could only get a clue. Anything pointing to one guy."

"How about the phone calls? You know the woman he got yesterday told us she'd gotten two strange calls last week from

11

a guy who fed her a lot of dirty talk. Maybe he pulls that with his other victims."

Goldberg nodded. "That could be. If we got tipped off that somebody was doing that, we might tap the girl's line and try to trace him. The only trouble is that, number one—the call might be from a crank; you know how many cranks call and frighten people whenever there's a prowler scare. Number two—it might be some boy friend with a weird sense of humor."

Farley shook his head. "But if the call were genuine it might be the lead we need. The call could tell us if the prowler knows his victims and their habits, or whether he just picks a name in a phone book. The trouble is that if he does call, ten to one she'll never report it. Probably think it a practical joke."

"Can we see the baby sitter he attacked yet," Goldberg asked.

"Still under sedation. She was a little unbalanced anyway, Abe."

The detectives did not notice a tall young man with a crew cut and wearing a sports jacket who moved quietly behind them.

"If this thing doesn't break soon, I may have a divorce on my hands," Goldberg said bitterly. "Every time this bastard strangles another girl, Becky looks at me as if I were responsible. As if I could have stopped it. She's sore about all the night work too. Who asked for this Goddamned case?"

"Don't take it so hard, Lieutenant," the man behind them said. He was kneeling by the girl's body, examining it. "You got the case because you solved those muggings in Harlem five years ago."

"Without turning I can tell you who that is," Goldberg said, scowling. "The great crime reporter." He turned quickly. "How'd you get up here so fast? I told them to keep you away till we finished."

"Come on, come on," Saxon said, grinning so that a little boyish cleft in his chin could be seen. "I'm sorry. No harm intended. Can I look around at least? This is my bread and butter."

Goldberg shrugged. "The trouble is it's hard not to like him," he told Farley as Saxon disappeared into the house.

"Better go easy," Farley cautioned. "He is a reporter."

"Yeah," Goldberg said, looking at the door Saxon had entered. Then he walked toward the house. "I'm going to watch that guy."

12

Saxon was reading a letter near the window. Goldberg took it out of his hands.

"Interesting," Saxon said. "She got letters from a very famous movie actor. About thirty years older."

Goldberg opened Saxon's jacket and took out three letters from the inside pocket. "You know I can haul you in for trying to steal."

"I wasn't stealing, just going to make notes."

Goldberg sighed. "I admire your guts, Harvey. But I feel like kicking you in the pants every time you do this."

"This is a very competitive town," Saxon said. "And the inspector said I could work close to you."

"You're close all right," Goldberg said. "Sometimes I almost feel you get there before I do." Saxon made a move as if he were being rapped on the knuckles with a ruler and Goldberg smiled. "Get out of here, you ham. I'll be in the office in an hour and give you what I know."

Saxon grinned. "I'm only trying to make a buck. And I hate the night shift. Can you blame me?"

"No. I'd just feel sorry for anybody you apply the needle to. There isn't anybody in L. A. who can smell a skeleton in a closet like Harvey Saxon."

"You're not too bad yourself, Lieutenant." Saxon left quickly after another look around. Goldberg watched him get into his '52 Jaguar and shoot down the hill. Then he walked over to Farley and said, "I've been thinking about that dirty phone call, Jim. It really may mean something. Especially if he called twice. It may be the prowler's pattern. The trouble is we can't be sure. We only have one witness who can talk. The others are all dead. I wish I knew if he called the baby sitter, for instance."

"I just hope that if he calls some girl again, the kid has enough brains to let us know right after it happens," Farley said.

2

THE NEXT TELEPHONE CALL from the man the newspapers later headlined as the Hollywood Prowler came on Monday, a few minutes before midnight.

Vita Reynolds had been waiting for two hours for John

13

Palmer to call and patch up the quarrel they had had in the office that morning. When the phone rang, she was sitting in the living room of her house in Hollywood, trying to get through Plato's *Republic* which was being discussed the next evening in her Great Books course. She had been trying hard to get through it for over an hour, but it was slow going. For ten minutes she had been paralyzed by one sentence.

To make herself more comfortable, Vita had put on the robin's-egg-blue silk nightgown John had given her for her twenty-sixth birthday and had curled up on the sofa beneath the big lamp with the global map shade. Her eyes kept returning to the sentence but her thoughts wandered.

She was hungry suddenly and she went into the small kitchen behind the living room, taking a short cut through her bedroom to do so. In the bedroom she paused at the bureau, filled with her perfume and cologne bottles, and stared moodily at the framed picture of John and herself. It had been made at the beach near Malibu three weeks earlier.

She decided for the fiftieth time that they made a good couple and that her small, thin dark face went well with his strong, aggressive one. Her five-foot-six-inch figure filled out her lavender bathing suit well, she decided, but the breasts were too prominent. On the other hand her legs looked good. They were long and well-shaped, tapering just right from her thighs. But the thighs seemed a little too thick to her now, though John had insisted they were not. She also felt she was just a little too thick in the hips.

In the kitchen, she looked through the shelves and could not decide what she wanted. Something light, she said to herself. It was nearly midnight. She passed over the tuna fish and the baked beans and the cans of succotash and boned chicken. Vita loved to stock up on everything that caught her eye on the shelves of the giant supermarket a few blocks away. She loved raiding the kitchen shelves late at night and making a snack of the most interesting items she could find.

Remembering the last stomach upset, three nights earlier, she started by selecting a can of sweet corn and some smoked oysters. But a second later she had grabbed a can of spaghetti and meatballs, a can of tomato paste and a small bottle of olive oil. She dumped a mixture of all three into a casserole and set it over a slow fire.

She heard a slight noise that seemed to come from upstairs, and wondered if her landlord had returned early. The Johnsons had told her they expected to be away making a film about three weeks. But occasionally Mr. Johnson, who

14

was a movie cameraman, flew back to Los Angeles to get new lenses or equipment. She listened for a moment, but there was no further noise. Probably mice, she thought, or the night breeze rattling the French windows. There had been no light when she came home that night and Mr. Johnson would have called if he were in to get his mail and messages.

Walter Johnson was a lanky, energetic man in his late thirties from St. Louis who loved to drink beer and gossip about his work. His wife was a pleasant, shy woman who seemed a little embarrassed by Walter's pep and occasional dirty jokes. They always invited Vita for dinner or beer and Welsh rabbit when they came back from a location trip. Walter was in great demand because he was an excellent color cameraman and particularly good in shooting close-ups of the sexier film stars.

Mary Johnson had assured Vita many times that she had never had any trouble with Walter in the woman department, and Vita decided he was probably no worse than some of the men from her firm who picked up girls in Chicago bars when they went there for conventions.

She looked at her wrist watch and saw that it was almost midnight.

The faint noises from upstairs had stopped.

Why didn't the idiot call? she wondered peevishly. She lit another cigarette and puffed at it nervously, wondering if she should call him. Vita liked to think she was unconventional, but her pride would keep her from calling a man at midnight. She knew she would lie awake for an hour, worrying about their quarrel. She wished she did not have such an adolescent temper, quick to read a slight into every phrase. John had told her lately he felt he had to walk on eggs when they talked. She knew what the oversensitiveness meant. She felt insecure and miserable because John had promised to ask his wife for a divorce and had been dragging his feet for weeks. He had logical reasons for dragging his feet, but she felt insecure anyway.

John's refusal to ask Ginny for a divorce because he was worried about losing most of his money and property, was their usual reason for quarreling. Another lesser one was her dates with Herbert Buhler, a boy from her home town whom she had known since childhood.

She picked up a copy of the *Readers Digest*. A minute later she put it down. Why the devil didn't he call? she thought, getting angrier by the minute. She tried thinking of a good, cutting phrase to spike him with when he finally did' get around to calling.

She snuffed out the stub of her cigarette. John could go to hell! But she wished he would call so she could tell him to. He was probably in his favorite Hollywood bar sulking about Buhler or pub-crawling along Sunset Boulevard with some of his hell-raising advertising chums. He had a hard, stubborn streak in him sometimes. He was unbelievably kind and understanding about most things and usually let her have her way. But he could not stomach Herbert Buhler.

Buhler was her oldest friend in Los Angeles, a boy who had gone to the same high school and college back home. He was the only child of one of the top bankers in Sioux City and could have moved right into his father's bank. Instead he had come to grips with the stubborn old man by insisting on becoming a minister. His ambition had always been to attend the Yale divinity school and later go into missionary work abroad. His mother, a frail, extremely religious woman, had encouraged him. But when she died, the elder Buhler, with a bull-like tenacity, had insisted that his son work in the bank for two years after leaving college. Herbert had complied, but he had been intensely miserable. Buhler Senior still opposed the idea of his becoming a missionary and had finally agreed to let Herbert go into teaching. It had taken his son two years to summon up enough courage to make the move to Los Angeles. His father had let him go only because he was ashamed to see him teaching in a local high school.

When Vita came to Los Angeles, her mother goaded her into joining Herbert's church group and spurred her into going steady with him. Vita had always found Herbert a little dull, but she knew no one else and, to please her mother, she had agreed. She let him take her to two church group meetings weekly, to a Great Books course where the classics were discussed and occasionally to his Sunday School class. As time went on, she could see that the tall, husky, blond schoolteacher was becoming strongly attracted to her, and she sensed in that intuitive way that some women have, that he was casting about for a chance to propose to her.

He occasionally kissed Vita good night at the door, slobbering over her lips in an excited schoolboy fashion, then jerking himself away and apologizing. But then Herbert's behavior had always seemed odd. She remembered once how his hand had "accidentally" covered her breast when he was helping her with her coat. His hand had lingered there in

16

what she had thought was a "pass," but a second later he had reddened and became so contrite she had felt sorry for him. He had made the same "mistake" many times when he helped her.

After that she had wanted to stop seeing him very often. But she knew her mother would be hurt. Vita's mother felt that as long as Vita was going around with a home-town boy, Los Angeles was safe. Moreover John was still stalling about getting a divorce and she felt it was wrong to see him exclusively.

John hated Herbert, whom he had met once or twice at her house. He hated Herbert's sanctimonious air, his conversation, which had strong Biblical overtones and often made him sound as if he were reciting a sermon, and his high-pitched tenor voice. He called Herbert "a wholesome pumpkinhead from the Corn Belt."

Herbert returned John's dislike with interest. He jeered that Palmer "reeked of corruption," and was a "slick Madison Avenue word-slinger."

3

THE TELEPHONE'S RINGING suddenly broke into her reverie. John, she thought excitedly, scooping the instrument impatiently from its cradle. "Hello, Mr. Madison Avenue," she said pleasantly, teasing him with a nickname she occasionally used when they laughed at Herbert. There was a long silence. "John?" she asked quickly, fighting to control her voice. "John, is that you?"

"Hello," a pleasant voice said finally. "How are you, Vita?"

Vita frowned. The voice seemed familiar, but she could not quite place it. It might be John faking. Sometimes, to amuse her, he mimicked Dennison, the gravel-voiced, tough executive director of the Stevens Dairy, or other people from the office. "Is this John Palmer?" she asked doubtfully.

"No, ma'am, it's not," the voice said pleasantly. "Is this Vita Reynolds?"

Her failure to place the voice despite it's irritating familiarity annoyed her.

"Well, will you please tell me who you are," she asked.

"Oh, just a friend. Someone who likes you very much," the

17

voice said gently. "I like your name too. Vita means life in Latin. Did you know that?"

"Well, who are you?" she repeated. She disliked people who played "guess who" games on the telephone. She had an impulse to hang up, but it was probably someone from the office or the church group and he would probably own up in a moment. She was sure she knew the person because the voice had a disturbingly familiar ring.

"Well say a few more words," she said patiently, "I'm sure I know you."

"Well you do, Vita. But I was betting myself you wouldn't recognize my voice."

She listened carefully. The voice had a high-pitched tenor quality. It seemed to come from a young man and it had a Middle Western flat tone. It sounded like many of the voices she had heard at home. In fact, she thought suddenly and triumphantly, it sounds quite a bit like Herbert Buhler. But what was Herbert doing calling at midnight? He generally went to bed early.

"Say something else," she begged, to be sure.

"Well, I think you're the prettiest girl in Hollywood and you've got a lovely figure. Always like looking at you, especially in the bright sunlight."

It was uncanny. It really did sound a lot like Herbert. It could be Herbert speaking through a handkerchief maybe or disguising his voice a little. Or drunk. The thought of Herbert drunk made her smile.

"Is this Herbert Buhler?" she asked doubtfully, thinking that he would probably sooner die than call an unmarried woman at midnight. Herbert took his position as a Sunday School Bible teacher very seriously and as far as she knew had absolutely no sense of humor.

"No," the voice said patiently and agreeably, "it is not Herbert Buhler. It is not Herbert anything. Just someone who admires you and thinks you beautiful. You have beautiful legs. Really beautiful legs. Has anyone told you how absolutely gorgeous your legs are?"

She smiled. It must be one of the men who worked in the advertising department. They knew she was interested in John Palmer, the advertising manager, and occasionally they teased her because she came to his office on flimsy pretexts. She remembered how one of John's colleagues had let loose a wolf's whistle one day when she had come by in a thin summer dress.

"I think I know who you are," she said smiling into the

18

phone. "But don't you think it's a little late for practical jokes?"

"Who am I?" the voice asked. It seemed a little disturbed by her question. "Are you really sure you know me?"

"Aren't you the red-headed boy who works on the third floor?"

"Maybe I am?" the man said slowly, "and then again, maybe not. It doesn't matter."

"Who are you?"

"I won't tell you. I just want you to know I love your legs. And your figure. You have a really lovely figure."

"Well thank you, sir," Vita said. "I didn't know you had noticed it." She was sure now that it was the red-headed boy—someone named Blakely. "You people always look so busy when I come in."

"Oh I'm never too busy to look at a beautiful woman." The voice was not joking. It was terribly earnest. "I love looking at you, Miss Reynolds. You have the longest, most beautiful legs I have ever seen on a girl. I love the way they peep out of those shorts, and the wonderful tan color."

Vita laughed. "Now you're just making things up. I've never worn shorts around the office, Mr.—Blakely, isn't it?"

"Maybe." The voice went on quickly. "Are you in love with anyone, Miss Reynolds?"

So that was it? The men in John's office were trying to smoke them out into the open. Vita smiled to herself as she listened.

"Whatever gave you that idea, Mr. Blakely?"

"Who's Mr. Blakely?" the voice asked, surprised.

"You. I know your voice. You're a tall red-headed man who works in John Palmer's office."

"Where?"

"In the Stevens Dairy naturally," Vita was getting annoyed. "I should think the least thing you could do is admit who you are. I mean if you're going to wake some girl up at this hour of the night."

The voice answered slowly, emphasizing each word. "I always call girls this hour of the night. I like to visit them this hour of the night, too. Everything's quiet. Just the girl and me. We're in a world of our own. I can hold you or kiss you without the telephone or the doorbell ringing."

"You really are a surprise," Vita said. "I thought you were the shy type, Mr. Blakely. I never expected this from you."

"I'm not Mr. Blakely." The voice sounded irritated now. "Stop calling me that."

19

Vita jumped. The voice sounded like Herbert's now. It had the same note of irritation when she stubbornly contradicted him.

"Speak a little more," she said, "I'm sure I know that voice. Especially when you get mad."

There was silence again broken only by a strange clicking noise. Finally Vita broke it.

"All right. I give up. Now please tell me who you are. Conversations like this drive me crazy. I know that I know you."

"Oh you don't know me. You may just think you do."

Now she had to know who this was. "Keep talking," she pleaded.

"About what?"

"Anything?"

"I could talk for hours about you. Especially those long, tanned legs and the strong tan thighs with the lovely white marks just where the shorts end. I bet you're lovely up beyond that too."

Her flesh began to crawl as she listened.

Vita blushed. Who on earth would talk to her that way? Would Blakely or Herbert? Suddenly she had it. It was John Palmer disguising his voice. She was relieved. Now the odd flavor of the conversation was explained. "Come out from behind that Iowa drawl, John," she said. "I know you. You had me worried for a while with that talk."

"My name's not John." The voice was amused now.

"Come on, John," she said. "I've had all I want of this cat and mouse game. I've been waiting hours for your call."

"Who's John, your boy friend?"

"Will you *stop*," she begged. "You can scare a girl to death, calling her at this hour and talking like that."

"I'm not John," he said. "I told you that. Who is he, your lover?"

Vita hung up, annoyed. What was the matter with him? Was he drunk? Couldn't he see she didn't think it was funny? How long could you carry on such an idiotic joke, with all the horrible stories about sex criminals attacking lonely women in Los Angeles.

She went to her bedroom and wet her forehead with a French cologne. Still cocking an ear for the phone, she browsed through the newspaper on the bed. The front page had a story about a prowler who had raped a young matron in Hollywood a day earlier. The big black headline screamed: *Sex Criminal Rapes Mother.*

Vita shivered a little as she read the story quickly. It told of how the landlady of an apartment building, half a mile from Vita's house, a young mother of twenty-eight had been mugged from behind. A man had attacked her while she was in her laundry room washing her clothes. The man had told her quietly he would kill her if she resisted. He had knocked her out with his fist. A neighbor who came down soon afterwards found her babbling incoherently. Suddenly as she finished the story, the telephone wailed across the room. Vita leaped to silence it.

"John," she shouted, almost crying with relief. "Darling, I'm sorry."

"You should be." Her heart sank. It was the same voice as before.

"John," she pleaded. "Are you sure this isn't you? Please, darling, let's stop this, if it is. I'm not amused any more."

"Vita, I swear to you this is not John Palmer," the voice said apologetically. "It's just someone who likes you very much."

Who was it then? Her mind raced over the possibilities. It could be any of several men she knew in the office.

"Well I give up," Vita said at last. "I don't know who you are. You could be any of a dozen people I know. Are you speaking your natural voice?"

"I think so," the voice said. "I'm surprised you didn't recognize me. But I guess you're sleepy."

"Well look, whoever you are. I think we'd better cut this short. You've won your bet or whatever started this business. I don't know you. You can tell me tomorrow and we'll both have a good laugh. Good night."

"Oh, don't hang up yet," the voice cut in, pleadingly.

"I'm too tired," Vita said, "and it's midnight."

"I love your voice," the man said. "It's as lovely as your body." He lingered over "body" in a way that made her blush.

"Well thank you," she said, trying to laugh in the spirit of the joke. "I think you must be a little drunk. Nobody ever says anything like that to me in the office."

"Well I'll call you tomorrow, if you'll give me your office number," the voice said helpfully. "Be glad to do it."

"I wish you'd tell me who you are," Vita said, a little exasperated now. "Do you work on my floor? Do we meet often?"

"Could be. You may not have noticed me," the voice said. "But I've noticed you all right. You've got a lovely face and a beautiful figure. It looks wonderful in that pink bikini bathing suit."

21

There was an awkward pause. "How do you know what I look like in a bathing suit?" Vita asked. Then it came to her. John had shown the photograph on the beach to everyone. She was foolishly pleased, and yet annoyed. Pleased because she wanted him to be proud of her. Annoyed because they had agreed not to publicize their relationship too much until his divorce came through.

"Oh I know. I've watched you. I know everything about you," the voice said slowly. "I know, for instance, that you have a little mole high up on your right thigh. I don't mind it, you understand, because you have lovely long legs and lovely thighs. I love it when you stretch out those lovely long legs and thighs and make love to the sun."

Vita felt her cheeks redden. "I don't think that's funny. It's in bad taste." The voice was working itself up to say more.

"I don't mind the mole at all. I don't even mind the freckles you have between your breasts. I don't mind because I love your breasts. They're beautifully shaped and they push so hard against your dress, I think they're coming through. I'd love to kiss them and bite them. Especially those hard brown tips. There are lots of other things under that dress I'd like to get my hands on."

The voice was beginning to alarm her now.

"If this is John, I think you're being disgusting."

"I'm not John, Vita," the voice corrected her affably.

She thought again, shivering, of the sex crimes that had been committed in the area and her blood ran cold. Should she hang up and call the police? She got a grip on herself quickly. This wasn't anything like that. The man had as good as admitted he worked with her or knew her. It had to be some horrible practical joke, and they would laugh themselves sick if she panicked and called the police. Probably they were hoping that she would do just that. But the idea that John was discussing her with men in the office as if she were some cheap pick-up who could be called up like this, was horrifying. Suddenly she felt very angry.

"Did John Palmer tell you to say these disgusting things?" she asked in a hard, resentful voice. She was sure now that they were all sitting in some bar on Sunset Boulevard, half-drunk, and that John was edging the speaker on. She felt sick and wanted to run to the toilet.

"Let me speak to Mr. Palmer," she said suddenly.

"He's not here, Vita," the voice said. "I told you that. What are you upset for? Just because I told you I want to bite your

22

beautiful breasts and run my hands up under your dress?"

She hung up and ran to the bathroom just in time. Afterwards she lay on the couch and cried into the pillow. How could John do such a horrible thing after telling her he loved her? How could she face those men in the office the next day, knowing John had boasted of his conquest, telling them the most intimate details about her. How could she work under those knowing smirks and snickers? She felt more wretched than she had ever felt in her life. She would never love anyone again.

But how could a man as decent as John do anything so disgusting? Trying to frighten a girl living alone by giving her all this filthy talk in the midst of a sex crime scare? She had known him only eight months, but she considered him the most sensitive, intelligent, decent man she had ever known, a man whose only flaw was a growing jealousy which secretly pleased her.

4

SHE LISTENED for the telephone to ring again but nothing happened. A faint, unrecognizable noise seemed to be filtering through the ceiling. She listened, trembling a little. But then it stopped. She felt better after she lit a cigarette and took several long pulls. Then she tried to put the weird phone conversation out of her mind.

For a moment she gave herself up to thinking about John Palmer and her feelings about him. Actually she was secretly flattered by his jealousy, though she did not like to admit this even to herself. She told everyone, herself included, that she hated possessive, demanding men, but she knew that the intensity of John's feeling, colored by his constant demands on her time and the way he showed his anger at her dates with Herbert, had drawn her strongly to him from the beginning.

It seemed to Vita that she fell in love with John the day she met him, a week after she came to work. Palmer had just flown back from New York and had called the girls to discuss the new nation-wide ads. As it happened the others were out so Vita went in to see him alone.

She was already rather curious about him, having been

thoroughly briefed by Alice Thomas, the tall, attractive New York girl who had come to Stevens from a food magazine in Manhattan. Alice kept up a lively interest in the private lives of the company's executives and knew all the dirt. Her acid comments on their efforts to promote what Alice called "intramural sex" enlivened most of their coffee breaks in the company cafeteria.

John Palmer had got his nose a little dented in an air crash in Korea. It made him look like a promising middle-weight. He was married to one of the most beautiful fashion models in New York, but was separated from her.

Vita noticed the resemblance to a boxer when she finally met Palmer. The slightly flattened nose, and the big, strong chin did suggest a fighter. But the large, soft brown eyes seemed the gentlest she had ever seen. He had smiled when she entered and put out his big hand in a friendly way. He was a tall, broad-shouldered man and he looked very sporty in his light homespun jacket. His dark crew cut made him look younger than his thirty-eight years. She had never seen anyone so restless. He'd moved about the room constantly as he talked, with a cigarette in his fingers. After discussing the ads with her, he'd said suddenly, "Let's go."

"Go where?" she'd asked confused.

"The bar at the Biltmore. I can't think in this place. I was weaned on Madison Avenue. I have to sit in a cool, dark room, sipping Martinis and pretend I'm near Radio City." He'd stopped and looked hesitant. "Will you let me buy you a drink, please?"

"I'd rather finish here," she said a little primly. Palmer was not her boss, but in a sense he was her superior.

"I'm not asking you up to my flat," he'd said teasingly. "I just asked you to step across the street."

She'd blushed, and he'd laughed at her discomfiture. "Don't ever give up blushing," he'd said softly. "You do it beautifully. Coming?"

She'd sat there feeling ridiculous and wondering what she ought to do.

He'd noticed her hesitation and sighed. "All right," he'd said, dropping the bantering tone. "So you're a new pretty girl in the office and I'm lonely and not exactly panting to return to my hot little apartment. I just felt like talking to somebody. Skip it. Come in at nine tomorrow and we'll finish this."

He'd sat at the desk again and bridged his eyes with his hand, though he was not in the direct sunlight. Something in the gesture had made her acutely aware of how lonely he was.

"I'd like a drink," she'd said suddenly.

He'd smiled at her.

They had said little until they were seated in the dark, cool cocktail lounge. He'd seemed grateful to her for just being there and they'd talked easily for nearly two hours. She had never felt so much at home with anyone. Many times when she'd caught him looking deeply into her eyes, she'd experienced a funny feeling as if something strange and wonderful were happening to her. She'd felt happy and embarrassed about it and was glad the room was dark so he could not read her feelings. On the bus going home, she'd sat as though in a trance and had to walk six blocks back to her usual stop.

Without any plan they had fallen into the habit of meeting almost daily—usually for a drink after work. But sometimes they would go on to long, talky dinners in an aromatic French restaurant or one of the lovely candlelit Mexican Cafés where nervous guitar music was played. On weekends John drove her to the ocean. Like many girls raised on the prairie, Vita could never get her fill of the endless blue sea and had to look at it at least once a week. John, who had grown up in Michigan, closer to blue water, was amused by her passion for the Pacific but took her often. They would lie in the sun for hours and then go on to the swank Holiday House motel in Malibu for cocktails and dinner.

She had been a little disturbed occasionally by John's passion for Martinis, but she'd known he was worried about the new promotion he was in line for. His growing possessiveness pleased her. He'd become quickly irritable and morose if they did not meet at least for lunch every day. And long before he'd asked her to be his wife at the Chicago conference, he'd become jealous of her evenings with Herbert Buhler.

John was reluctant to intrude his marital troubles into their budding relationship, but she could tell how depressed the waiting had made him by the sadness in his voice.

"The hell of it," he told her, "is that Ginny doesn't really care whether we divorce or not. All she's got on her mind is some damned television deal she's been trying to get for weeks. They've offered her the part of a nun who helps lost kids in some new TV series and her agent's dickering with them now. It's the biggest thing she's ever had a smell at and she can't think of anything else. I laughed when she told me. Ginny not only loathes children—she hasn't seen the inside of a church since we were married.

"Anyway," he'd said wistfully, looking at her sadly, "I feel like the original dangling man. That's one reason I've fought shy of relationships like this. I know how easy it is to let yourself enjoy the kicks of a rebound love. It's so pleasant to have your ego massaged by a pretty girl when it's been so painfully flattened. I've tried hard to avoid using you that way."

She'd known what he'd meant. They had been seeing one another almost daily for several weeks but he had never tried to go to bed with her.

"In a way I'm sorry I started this," he'd continued quietly, looking deeply into her eyes. "I've had no dates of any kind in weeks. If my wife ran into me with a pretty girl or if her friends ran into me, I think she'd dig her feet in against going on with the divorce. You know, dog in the manger stuff.

"I didn't know I was going to look forward to being with you so much or get such a kick out of nutty little things like watching you act like a baby whenever you see the ocean."

"I didn't know I was either," she'd said, kissing him. "I thought from what Alice said you were going to try to drive me up to some motel in Palm Springs like some of the executives around here are supposed to."

"Oh, I never would have picked Palm Springs. That would be like having a seduction in a goldfish bowl," he grinned. "I'd pick a cabin in the hills."

A disquieting thought came to her a moment later.

"If you've waited six months for a divorce don't you think you may still love her?" she'd asked.

"No," he'd said, his face hardening, "that's over." He'd paused and then he'd said slowly, "We never had too much really. I mean it was never a great success as a marriage. But what really killed it was her refusal to have another child. She had a miscarriage with our first and after that she just flatly refused to have another. There was no medical reason," he'd said bitterly. "She just didn't want a child, and I wanted one more than anything else in the world."

He'd flushed and changed the subject quickly, as if he'd been afraid of boring her or as if he'd seemed ashamed to air his longing for fatherhood.

That night, when he'd brought her home, he'd kissed her impulsively in the car. It was not much of a kiss at first. They had parked and he had turned off the headlights to have a cigarette with her as usual before leaving. He had never asked or been asked to come in. Suddenly as he'd bent over to light her cigarette, he'd pulled it from her lips and kissed her softly. She'd overcome her surprise and responded.

26

The thing that worried John most was whether he was going to get the sales job that was coming up at Stevens. He and Vita quarreled about his fears that a messy divorce might ruin his chances.

Thinking of it now, Vita wondered if she would not have been better off if she had broken with John in the beginning. She had long ago told herself that she would not think about marriage with him, that if it happened one day, fine. And he had not even attempted to make love to her until they had gone together to Chicago.

Suddenly, as she sat thinking about John, a sharp odor of burning hit her nostrils. The spaghetti and meatballs! She rushed to the kitchen but it was too late. The bottom of the casserole was covered with a technicolored goo which resembled boiling red tar. She sighed and decided to clean the pot the next day. Opening the refrigerator, she selected a pear, took a few bites and then, still wondering about the telephone call, she went to bed.

5

WHEN VITA HAD COME to Los Angeles, it had been the first major trip of her life, the first away from her family. When she worked for the state government in Des Moines, her mother had lived with her. Later, when she worked as assistant to the food editor on a Minneapolis newspaper, her mother had joined her. The job in Los Angeles had come as a result of a trip west for the newspaper. Like many Iowans, she had fallen in love with Southern California at once. The week she spent there amidst the palm trees, the constant sunshine, the swimming pools and the terraced estates, had been the most exciting week she had spent in her entire life. She had instantly been bewitched by the easygoing place, the informality of dress.

When the head of the home economics department of the dairy concern told her there was a vacancy she could fill, she'd accepted immediately.

The apartment Vita loved even more than her job. She had felt at home in it at once. It was in the rear of an old frame house set back on one of the quiet streets that curled in a lazy fashion up the gentle foothills north of Sunset Boulevard. Vita had dreaded the thought of living in one of the crowded eight-or sixteen-unit apartment buildings that housed so many bachelors in Los Angeles.

Vita's mother had stayed with her for a short time and had then returned to Iowa. She planned to sell their house and return to Los Angeles to be with Vita permanently. Meanwhile she worried about Vita constantly and depended on Buhler to keep an eye on her. Mrs. Reynolds had a heart condition and Vita was always careful not to excite her.

Vita had refused her mother's plea to give up the flat while she was away and to live with one of the girls. She was used to letting her mother have her way, but more and more her independence was beginning to assert itself in Los Angeles. She knew her mother would violently disapprove of John and so had told her nothing about him.

Three days a week she worked at home on the commercials for her company's daytime television show. It was John who had suggested it. Vita loved the idea. She did the commercials about the different Stevens products quickly and then she would lie around the house doing odd chores. Or she would get a blanket and take sunbaths on the fingernail of green lawn behind the house, leaving the back door open so she could hear the phone.

Whether it was the climate, or the promise of a better life, few people left Los Angeles, Vita knew. When the malcontents thought of their homes in the East, they remembered cold, frosty mornings when the breath hung heavily around their lips, when their cars would not start and the thick snow bottled up the front doors and had to be scraped from sidewalks. Or they remembered wet, gray afternoons after the watery, thin sunlight waned.

The excitement of the strange phone call had left her very clear-eyed and wakeful. It was all a bad joke, she decided, closing her eyes. But a seed of doubt would not be crushed. A news announcer on the radio had asked women who received such calls from strangers to inform the police. But she was sure this was not a stranger. And even if it were, she shuddered at the thought of getting involved with the police and having her name all over the newspapers and television news programs. She had seen pictures of women involved in such stories in the newsreel. They all had such an embarrassed, hunted look, as if they themselves had committed a crime, and were being pilloried for it. She did not want anything like that.

The next day, Vita waited impatiently for the mysterious caller to make his presence known. She watched alertly for a tell-tale smile or a tongue-in-cheek sally that would give the joker away. She was so edgy finally that she suspected several men of smirking knowingly when they greeted her warmly or smiled in the hall. She waited in vain for the caller to telephone, but nobody did. Nobody even referred to the call. A few times she almost mentioned it to the girls in the office, but she stopped herself. How could she repeat the details of the call to Helen Wright for instance? Helen, who supervised her section, was a woman of nearly fifty who had worked for the state of Minnesota for twenty years as a home economist and was easily shocked even by the slightly salty remarks of Alice Thomas.

It was a pretty full afternoon, and Vita was busy finishing an article about the uses of milk in cooking which a woman's magazine editor had requested. She had little time to think about either John or the mysterious telephone call until the coffee break at three-thirty. In addition to her article, Vita had to call newspapers to give food editors information.

The office was a small but pleasant room with high ceilings which overlooked Pershing Square in downtown Los Angeles. There were three desks in the room, each near a window— Vita's, Alice's, and one belonging to Claire Bronson. Claire was a specialist in radio material and had come to the firm from a little radio station in Texas. She was a mousy woman with a narrow face and a tall, gaunt figure. Her hair was a brown mass which seemed to embarrass her because she changed her hairdo every week or two, either wearing it in a chignon that made her look like a grim, determined schoolteacher, or long, which made her look only sad.

She had been married once, unsuccessfully, and it had soured her permanently on men. Since she was nearly the same age as Helen, she generally patronized the younger girls. Alice could not endure her and spoke to her as little as possible, except when a common irritation with the advertising manager, John Palmer, or a peculiar whim of Helen's made them reluctant allies. Vita did not dislike her, but could not warm to her. But since Claire was a member of her church group and knew Herbert Buhler, she could not avoid her. Claire knew her work well and turned out excellent food material for women's radio programs, but her complete lack of humor and her determination to defend her chastity against males, all of whom she was certain wanted to sleep with her, made her a trying person to work with.

29

Vita worked on her article for two hours, but the strange call kept coming back to her thoughts. She still suspected that John Palmer had engineered the whole thing, and she was irritated by his failure to speak about it. When the coffee break came, Vita decided to speak to John whether he liked it or not. She rose from her desk and started determinedly from the room.

John Palmer rose embarrassedly from behind his desk when she strode in. He had been talking to his assistant, Tom Blakely. The big advertising manager's eyes looked wary and a little hurt as they met hers. For a moment she wished Blakely would leave so she could have it out with him alone. It hurt her terribly when she saw that pained look in John's eyes and knew that she was partly to blame.

"I don't know how to say this," she began worriedly. John's eyes suddenly filled with concern. He shot a quick glance at his red-haired assistant, who got up to go.

"No, wait a minute—this concerns you too," she said.

"Sit down, Vita." John said softly. The familiar warm grin began to grow around the corners of his mouth. He was glad she had come now. He had been on the verge of calling her several times after lunch. Vita sat down coolly.

"Did you call me at midnight last night, Mr. Blakely?" she asked, looking at him carefully.

Blakely looked astonished and stared at his chief. "No."

"Are you sure?" she said ruthlessly.

"Of course. Why on earth should I call you at midnight?"

"I don't know. It might have been your idea of a pretty funny practical joke. Some people think it's pretty funny to call a girl in the middle of the night and give her an earful of dirty talk."

"Not me," Blakely said firmly.

"It sounded a little like you," Vita said. "I wouldn't have enjoyed it any night. But last night, with a sex criminal loose in the neighborhood, it nearly drove me out of my mind."

"Did you call Miss Reynolds," John said angrily.

"No," Blakely said worriedly. "I've never called her."

Vita shook her head unbelievingly. "It sounded like you, and whoever called said a lot of things that only one other person knew about me." She stared coldly at John. "It was something only Mr. Palmer knew and which he could have passed on to you."

"Now wait a minute, Vita," John interposed, "that's out of line. I haven't passed on anything to anyone. Who was this man? Did he pretend to be Mr. Blakely?"

"No, he didn't give his name. He just kept giving me a lot of the filthiest language I've ever heard. It's so horrible I can't even repeat it. But I know it must have been someone who got it from you. He couldn't have known those things otherwise. He knew all about how I looked in a bathing suit for instance and," she blushed, "about certain other things."

Blakely looked unhappy. "I assure you it wasn't me, Miss Reynolds. I'd never pull a thing like that in a million years. I was home all night with my family and I was asleep by eleven-thirty."

There was a tense silence while John searched his assistant's face, then Blakely made his excuses and left.

"I think that was a pretty awful thing to do, John," she said, annoyed. "To show him our beach photos and tell him about the freckles on my body, after you promised not to."

John's face looked bland. "What pictures? I never showed those pictures to anyone." He put his hands on her shoulders and said softly, "I'm telling you the truth, darling. I never showed those pictures to anyone." His deep voice was full of honest concern.

She looked at him through tear-filled eyes. "You didn't show the pictures to anyone? You're absolutely certain?" He hesitated. "Don't soft-soap me, John. I want to know. If this is a joke, I'm not enjoying it. Whoever called me talked to me as if I were a prostitute. I've never heard such filthy talk in all my life. I had to throw up afterward."

"It must have been a drunk who got your number by accident, honey. Those things happen all the time." He kissed her gently on the lips after a quick glance at the door.

"You're sure no one saw those pictures?"

After a slight hesitation he nodded quickly. "Nobody did."

"And it wasn't you impersonating anyone?" She looked pleadingly at him. "Darling, tell me if it was. I'd feel much much better about it. I wouldn't mind really. Especially if it was you. The thing that makes me nervous is that there are so many prowlers around. Especially in my neighborhood. Several women have been attacked in the last three weeks and a girl was killed only ten blocks away. I couldn't sleep all night thinking about this thing."

"Don't worry about it, darling. It's probably just some silly drunk who called up from a bar in Hollywood. If you hadn't read all this stuff in the papers, you'd have laughed it off." He kissed her. "Now give us a grin and get back to work before Blakely tells the whole world you've been spending the afternoon here."

Vita smiled. "Thanks, darling. And forgive me."

"Look, suppose I come over tonight and keep you company," he said. His brown eyes watched her expectantly.

Her eyes lit up and then changed. "I'd love that, John. I'd love that more than you know. But tonight's the church social meeting. I've got to go. I'm head of the arrangements committee for the pageant."

John shook his head. "Call it off. Let Buhler carry it for you."

She shook her head. "I can't, John. Let's make it tomorrow."

"Tomorrow, tomorrow!" John Palmer looked angry. "Every time I want to see you I've got to lose you to the pumpkinhead. Just because your mother might get a nasty letter. I'm getting damned sick of it."

"John, I'm sorry. But I just can't get off tonight. It's got absolutely nothing to do with Herbert. I just am in too deep and I can't throw my whole private life away just because you want me to. I haven't demanded that you divorce your wife."

She saw his face change. "I'm sorry, John."

"It's not the same thing, Vita," he retorted. "I've got to play it Ginny's way or I may lose my shirt. This is California. I've told you how the community property law works, damn it. I'm trying to get her to take less than half of everything I own. If she takes half, there isn't going to be much left for us to start on."

"Well, save your breath," she retorted, "and forgive me for disturbing you." She moved quickly through the doorway and slammed it. She marched to her room and sat down at her desk without a word to the girls.

"Does this mean war between the Consumer's Division and the advertising office?" Alice asked kittenishly. "Or has the newspaper story upset you?"

"What story?" asked Claire, who was following the conversation carefully.

Alice lifted the afternoon newspaper from her desk and showed her the front page. A huge black headline read:

PROWLER STRIKES AGAIN
ACTRESS KILLED IN HOLLYWOOD

Vita looked at her. "What's that got to do with me?" she asked, wondering if Alice knew about the call.

"Nothing, except it's in your neighborhood, dear. Just a few houses away. He strangled a girl in her garden. And police say they're sure it's the same man who's been operating in the area before. Here, read it yourself."

Vita did not want to read the story, but was afraid to refuse.

She took the newspaper from Alice. The story ran over two columns on the right-hand side of the front page.

> The slaying of a lovely young Hollywood actress who had apparently been strangled by a prowler brought scores of calls for protection today from frightened housewives in the Hollywood area.
>
> According to police, Carol Forsythe, 24-year-old actress under contract to a prominent studio, was sunning herself in the garden of her house in the Laurel Canyon area when the prowler struck.
>
> Police said they recognized evidence of the prowler who has already attacked six women within a mile radius and who may have murdered Lena Warner ten days ago. They described the prowler as a dangerous sex criminal who probably needs psychiatric care badly, but is not aware of it.
>
> Police warned women in the area to notify them immediately if they notice any strange or suspicious persons loitering nearby or if they receive anonymous telephone calls from anyone who flirted over the wire.
>
> Three of the women who were attacked or threatened in the Hollywood area said they had been called several times by a strange man who spoke insultingly on the telephone. None of the three had reported the call before their attack.

Vita felt her legs tremble as she gave the paper back to Alice. She sat down in her chair without a word, feeling very faint.

"Holy cow," Alice said. "You're not scared because of all that hooey, are you?" She laughed raucously. "Probably no damned connection at all. Probably three different guys too."

"I'm not scared," Vita answered quietly. She knew she was lying. The story had frightened her badly. Yet she was not completely satisfied that the call had not been a joke: how else could anyone explain the business about the bathing suit or the freckles? Unless it was Herbert? She fought a desire to call John and ask him to keep her company that night, to stay with her all night if necessary. But she drove it out of her mind. After their words a little earlier, she couldn't bear to knuckle under that way. Also, Herbert might not leave her until late and John would be furious. She could not put up with another jealous scene—not tonight. If only John would admit Blakely had done it and had seen the beach photograph everything would be simple. Unless she knew the call had come from him, she knew there would be no sleep later. She would be in a constant terror of the phone ringing —of hearing last night's voice.

6

IN HIS OFFICE John stared quietly at the prowler story in the newspaper. Then he opened his top desk drawer and removed the beach pictures. He had lied to Vita. Blakely had seen them. One afternoon he had walked in unannounced and found John looking at them. Blakely had whistled and smiled understandingly, but had sworn to tell no one.

Now John wondered if Blakely was up to something. Had he called Vita the night before? Maybe he should have a talk with Blakely.

But his whole line of thought was silly. He was getting morbid, watching too many hackneyed television programs. Vita had just got some drunken crank, calling from a plush saloon on the Sunset Strip. And all that stuff about her bathing suit was just what a leering drunk might invent.

He sighed and looked at the pictures again. He was in love with this girl, he thought. Really in love. It wasn't just the old chemical routine this time. She was a wonderful girl and everything about her delighted him—even that awful cornbelt naïveté, even the occasional Sunday school teacher primness, even with that ghastly attempt at lovemaking in Chicago. He loved her and he would marry her if Ginny would only let go.

At four-thirty, he could not bear the thought that Vita was still annoyed. He called her. She answered too coolly, unwillingly revealing her anxiety about him.

"Meet me in the darkroom in five minutes, darling," he whispered.

"Why?" she asked. "I think we talked the whole thing out."

"Oh for Pete's sake, meet me," he begged. "I've been miserable ever since you left. Don't make me get on my hands and knees. I will if you don't. I'll come right down to that brothel you work in and tell those harpies you work with that I'm sick with love."

She laughed. "Oh shut up. I'll be there. What about the photographer? Isn't he there?"

"I sent him to Pasadena for the afternoon. Come on!"

"All right, but I don't think it's a good idea. People come up there all the time."

"Not this afternoon," he said hanging up. He felt suddenly exultant as he plunged down the back stairs to the photographer's workroom. He was at the back of a dark corridor lined with packing cases. He opened the door with the extra key he carried and put on the red warning light to keep people out. A moment later he was joined by Vita. He closed the door behind her and took her greedily into his arms. He moved back against the rear counter of the laboratory in the darkness and kissed her hungrily for several minutes.

"Aren't you going to put the light on," she asked when she caught her breath.

He turned on the red work light which gave the small room a garish, nightmare atmosphere. "It hardly improves you," he said drily.

"Did you ask me here for that?" she said, annoyed.

"No, I want to apologize. I shouldn't have brought up Buhler again."

"No, you shouldn't have," Vita chewed her lip a moment. "John, since we brought him up, I wanted to tell you that I want to break off with him anyhow. He's been acting strange and too possessive lately. But you'll have to be a little patient. I just can't afford to hurt Mother needlessly."

He nodded. "I know. And, darling, please don't think I'm dragging my feet about Ginny. I was going to ask her again tomorrow."

"How about that business deal with your friend in New York?"

He winced. Some time ago he had told her that a college friend had invited him to go into a small public relations agency in New York, as a full partner.

"Darling, I need more time to consider that."

"Why? It sounds wonderful. You'll be your own boss and I can help too. You told me I could handle several home economics accounts for food companies. And the beauty of it is, you don't have to worry about your wife's ruining anything. You're terrified of her now because she may drag you through the mud and kill your chances of a promotion here."

"I know, I know," he said wearily. They had talked it out half a dozen times. "But I can't take home more than five thousand a year from the agency until it's on its feet. Now I'm making three times that. And if I play along I can become Western sales manager in two years. I'll be making twenty-five thousand to start. Can you understand that, darling?"

"I can only understand that you're obsessed with money," she said despondently. "Maybe we ought to forget the whole thing. Maybe you ought to get yourself another girl. I'm not sure I fit into the Caddy class."

"I don't want another girl," he said softly, "so dry up. I love you."

"I don't know why," she said. "We're always squabbling, and I act like a silly virgin whenever you make love to me."

"I love you because you're the most opposite it's possible to be from Ginny. You're a little naive—" she tried to break away but he held her close, laughing—"no don't get mad. I love you because you are naive. I'm so sick of modern girls darling. You try to sound terribly modern sometimes, so blasé about sex and male-female relations, and yet I know you're absolutely terrified about sex."

"And that makes you love me?" she asked wonderingly.

"No. Not that. But what happened in Chicago. Knowing how terrified you were when you let me come to you—" He kissed her hungrily. "Oh, you know what I mean."

"Yes, but sometimes I'm not sure if I am good for you, John," she said slowly. "We're so different. You're so hot-headed about everything. You never plan anything out. You just get a flash and want to jump into something. I'm not like that. I never could be."

"I know," he said gently, holding her close. "And that's why I need you. I need someone like you to ride herd on me. To keep me in line. To get me organized. Listen, I love everything about you. I love you because you're beautiful and good, and I can't get you out of my mind."

"I know," she said. "I know. You've told me a hundred times why you love me, darling. I just can't believe it, that's all. I'd believe it if you got that damned divorce. If you stopped talking about it and just did it."

He looked unhappy. "I will," he promised. "She'll come

around in a week or so. I know it. Please just be a little patient." He kissed her. "I'll make it up to you. And I've had to be a little patient too," he reminded her.

He held her close and ran his lips softly down her throat until she shivered with excitement. He moved his lips to hers and moved his fingers tenderly along the lobes of her small, delicate ears. He could feel her excitement mounting and her face growing warm next to his.

As she leaned over the big table, her skirt rose and he could see a few inches of bare flesh above her stocking tops. He felt himself flush with excitement. But a small warning voice held him back. He could possess her right there on the table, he knew. She was burning with desire and her forehead was glistening with sweat. He pushed her back gently against the table and raised her skirt above her knees. She let him move her silently, staring at him with widened eyes. A second later he stopped.

"I'm sorry," he said simply. He kissed her, holding her erect and tightly to him so that he could feel her firm breasts hard against his chest. Without thinking his fingers began to tease her breasts from the outside and caress her throat and face.

"I can't stand it when we fight," he said miserably, closing her mouth before she could speak. "I'm sorry I brought up Buhler." He pressed her even closer as they leaned against a large worktable.

"Darling," she said, and ran her fingers through his hair. A wave of desire engulfed him and he could not prevent himself from touching the warm flesh under the skirt. He pressed his mouth hard against her hers and ran his tongue fiercely into it. His fingers moved excitedly under her dress. Suddenly he felt her trembling frightenedly and withdrew.

"I'm sorry, baby," he apologized. "I lost my head." She kissed him. "No. It's my fault. I thought I was over it."

"You don't lose a fear of sex overnight," he said softly. "Don't worry about it. It's my fault. I can't stand it when I'm near you. I want to touch you."

"I've got to get over it," she said adamantly.

"Darling, I had nothing to do with the phone call last night. I swear it. I couldn't play that kind of joke."

"I know," she said, "I just had to ask."

"If Blakely is pulling anything like that, I'll break his neck."

"It may not be him," she said. "It could be anyone. It was just so horrible, John."

"Don't worry about it, darling. It's probably just some stu-

37

pid crank." Inside, he was not sure and he felt a small bubble of fear forming. "I'll call you later to tuck you in," he promised.

Herbert Buhler called his class to order and told them to start their written test on the anatomy of mammals. He felt nervous about his date with Vita that evening and kept repeating the words he wanted to say. If she defended Palmer, he had to be firm—remind her that she was a decent Christian girl and had a duty toward her mother. He would remind her of her mother's heart condition and what news of her dating Palmer would do to her. He would try to make her see the difference between a decent church-going man who had never loved anyone else, who did not drink or smoke, and a Madison Avenue slick artist who neglected his wife and drank constantly.

A movement in the first row distracted his thoughts. It was that Green kid again. Carlotta Green. Every time she came in wearing those tight skirts and a tight jersey he found it impossible to lecture. She was a dark shapely fifteen-year-old with long tanned legs, large pointed breasts, robust thighs and a sensual mouth. Her dark eyes seemed always to be filled with boredom yet they followed him around the room as if they couldn't bear to let him out of their sight. The girl made him acutely uncomfortable. He had wanted to tell her to wear decent dresses, but this was Los Angeles, not Iowa. People just didn't care about those things.

He stole a quick glance at her. She was staring at him, but when she caught his glance, she looked down at her paper. Next to her, her bosom friend, Joan McNulty, was smiling as if she knew a guilty secret. The McNulty girl at least dressed properly. Her mother had some sense. Carlotta Green's mother must be something like her daughter, Herbert thought, too well-endowed and a little immoral. She never signed the girl's report card. It was usually an uncle who did.

Carlotta suddenly stretched her arms over her head and sighed. The gesture made her large breasts jut forward and despite himself, Herbert found himself looking at them. His eyes met hers and he found himself reddening. He wondered if he could get her to transfer to another class.

He looked down at the book he was reading. It was no use. Every time Carlotta moved her body, he was distracted. The McNulty girl could see his discomfiture too. Looking at her reminded him again of Vita. She lived on the same block; he remembered from her registration card.

38

He began to think of the words he wanted to say to Vita when he noticed that Carlotta had let her thighs open several inches. She was wearing no stockings. And her skin was a rich, light brown color. He could not help noticing how the color remained the same even under her skirt. Unless he kept his eyes glued to the book on his desk, he could not avoid looking at her-firm brown thighs. He wanted to leave the room but he had to proctor the examination.

He read the book for a while without looking up, but he couldn't do that for a whole hour. He would have to watch the class. His eyes returned involuntarily to Carlotta. Her legs seemed even wider apart now. When his eyes met hers, they seemed to have an understanding smile. Now she turned in her seat so that her hip was etched sharply under the tight skirt.

Suddenly he hated her. He had an impulse to pull her out of the seat and slap her. She was obviously baiting him and enjoying it enormously. In Sioux City he would have sent her home instantly. Here he could only look on and feel helpless. There was something impure and sinful about so many of these high-school girls who had no parental supervision. Wasn't that why there were so many cases of illegitimate pregnancies in the city schools? He made a mental note to speak to Reverend Michael about it at the church group meeting that evening.

It was impossible to look away. Again and again his eyes returned to Carlotta Green's long, shapely legs and the tantalizing glimpse of her bare thighs that her posture afforded. Occasionally, as if by accident, the girl lifted her eyes from her test paper and gazed at him. He knew she was aware of his interest in her legs, but she did nothing to rearrange her skirt or change her position. Instead she stretched out lazily, sensually, giving him a better view. Once she leaned back, almost too casually and he received a provoking, disturbing glimpse of her upper´thighs and he realized, his temples throbbing, that she wore no underpants. He reddened and turned away, furious with both her and himself. But a moment later he was staring with an almost hypnotic fixity at the girl's legs.

His indignation with Carlotta nearly choked him. She was a kind of Mary Magdalene that existed everywhere for the express purpose of corrupting decent Christian men. He decided to talk to her about dressing properly. California customs or not, he would have decency in his class. He looked guiltily at the girl's exposed legs, now blatantly open, and bit his lip. When the class bell rang, he said sharply, "Will Miss Green please stay for a moment after class. I have something to discuss with her."

Joan McNulty looked surprised and a little worried. But Carlotta smiled back placidly. "Wait for me in the yard, Joanie," she said.

Joan went to the yard and waited. Fifteen minutes later Carlotta came out with her books under her arm and smoking a cigarette.

"Holy smoke, put that out," Joan warned. "You know you can't smoke here."

Carlotta took a few more puffs unconcernedly and snuffed the cigarette on the brick wall. "To hell with them. If I feel like smoking, I ain't gonna worry about these monitor slobs."

"What happened with Mr. Buhler. What did he want to see you about?"

Carlotta gave her a knowing smile. "Guess."

"He probably told you to wear a wider skirt and a bigger sweater. I caught him staring at your legs the whole hour."

Carlotta gave her a bored smile. "He wasn't just staring at them. He was staring between them. I wasn't wearing anything underneath, that's why."

Joan was shocked. "Why not?"

"It's too damned hot, that's why. My mother never wears them either."

"Yes, but you were inviting him to look up your skirt, the way you kept wiggling around in that seat. I saw you."

"Sure," Carlotta said, "I wanted him to. I'm sick and tired of his Goddamned sermons on morality and decency and chastity. I decided to find out if he was a man or just a bag of wind. So I let him look."

Joan stared at her. Carlotta made her uneasy when she talked this way. But her curiosity got the better of her. "Did you find out?"

Carlotta smiled again. "What do you think?"

"No kidding," Joan said. "He propositioned you?"

"They're all alike. My mother told me that years ago. They all want one thing. They'll talk around the subject for hours and they'll yap about decency. But all they want to do is get in your pants. I know."

"You mean he really asked you. I don't believe it," Joan said. "Not him."

Carlotta shrugged. "I'm going up to his place after school. He's picking me up about a mile from here. Then we're having tea at his place."

40

"I still can't believe he'd try to go to bed with you," Joan said.

Carlotta looked annoyed. "Yeah? Is that why, when he asked me to come up, he moved his hand up my leg while I was standing next to his desk?"

7

AT NINE O'CLOCK that evening, Vita knew she could not endure the hot meeting room of the Hollywood church another moment. She caught Herbert's eye and then rose. The young pastor looked surprised.

"I'm sorry, Reverend Michaels," she said. "I've got a headache and didn't sleep much last night. Please don't bother, Herbert. I can catch a bus."

But Buhler had already left his seat. He took Vita's arm firmly. As they walked out, she could see Claire Bronson looking at her enviously. For the first time she began to realize the depth of the older woman's loneliness and decided to treat her more kindly. She wished there were even some way to get Herbert to take her out on evenings when he did not see her.

In the dark car Herbert put his arm about her protectively. "It was sticky in there," he said understandingly. He pulled her close for a minute and planted a slobbery kiss on her lips. She drew away impatiently.

"I know why," he said morosely. "You've been out too late with your friend Palmer. Probably out with him all night, sitting in some stuffy nightclub."

"Herbert," she began irritably, "don't start on *that* topic again tonight, for God's sakes."

He flushed. "Don't take the name of the Lord in vain, just because I'm trying to help you. You've lost a lot of weight and your color is awful." She jerked the handle of the door and jumped out. He leaped after her and pulled her arm. "I'm sorry," he said. "Let me take you home, please."

"Not if you're going to talk like that," she shot back.

He nodded miserably. "I can't help it sometimes. You know how I feel."

When she returned to her seat, she pulled nervously at the catch of her purse to get her cigarettes. Because she was so nervous, she dropped it. Everything spilled to the floor. Herbert bent to pick up her lipstick, keys and some loose coins. A couple of times she felt his hot forehead against her bare legs as he groped for things. The feeling of his close-shaven cheek against her bare calf a moment later made her shiver.

He seemed to take hours hunting for things and kept brushing against her legs even when she moved them aside to give him room.

When he returned to the wheel, his face was flushed and perspiring. Vita looked sympathetic. "I'm sorry, Herbert."

"That's all right," he said slowly, not looking at her. He brushed his blond hair back and drove away, his eyes glued to the road. When they arrived at her house, he helped her out of the car. For a split second she caught a strange look in his eyes as her skirt slid above her knees. He raised his eyes quickly.

A moment later when they were inside she asked slowly if he had called her at midnight the evening before. She told him a little about the call.

He was incredulous.

"You don't think I could do a thing like that?"

"Please forget it," she said hurriedly, "and don't write to my mother about it please. She'll just be scared to death."

Herbert wore the injured look he always wore when she told him not to mention anything to her mother.

"Do I still get my cup of coffee?" he asked in a hurt voice. "Even if I did get you angry?"

For a second, looking at his face, she wanted to laugh. Six-feet-three Herbert Buhler resembled a halfback with his broad shoulders and bull-like neck. On his face now was the penitent expression of an Airedale that has committed an unforgivable offense.

"Herbert," she began wearily, "I'm so sleepy."

"I want to discuss this call," he said petulantly. "Who was it? Have you any idea?"

"I don't know," she said. "It sounded a little like you. But it could have been someone in the office. Whoever it was knew a lot about me."

"It wasn't me," Herbert said firmly. "I don't call girls at midnight." He stared at her thoughtfully. "Vita, are you in any trouble with Palmer? Do you think it has anything to do with him?"

She blushed. "No," she said slowly, "I don't think so."

"People don't play jokes like that. Calling women at midnight and saying things like that unless—" Herbert blushed.

"Unless what?" Vita's face hardened.

"Well, all I meant was it's hard to swallow, that's all."

"What did you mean when you said unless?"

"Oh, I didn't mean anything, I guess." Herbert looked embarrassed as he reached into a fruitbowl on the table near the sofa and chose an apple. "It's just that things like that happen because men get ideas from girls."

Vita stood up angrily. "I think you'd better get out of here. Now."

"Ah, Vita. All I meant is maybe Palmer was a little drunk."

Her voice was furious. "It was not John Palmer."

"Well, who was it then?"

"I don't know, damn it. Don't you understand? It could have been anyone. It could have been that prowler they have all over the newspapers."

Herbert looked at her quietly for a moment. Then he shook his head and laughed. "Don't think that way, Vita. Don't jump to anything like that."

"I'm not jumping to anything," Vita retorted. "The papers say he's committed several attacks right in this neighborhood."

Herbert shook his head and grinned. "All I'm saying is, don't fly off the handle. Just because of all this fuss about a prowler, don't go looking under the bed and losing all kinds of sleep about it. It probably has nothing to do with it."

Herbert's bland composure irritated her as it always did at times like these. Herbert could never take any of her fears or worries seriously. Now his superior grin was maddening. He edged over to her side of the sofa and put his arm around her shoulder protectively. She moved away.

"I'm not flying off the handle," she said, "and I'm not losing any sleep. I'm—I'm just curious, that's all. I mean I never received a call like that." She looked at him carefully. "It's funny you suddenly think it's so amusing. Are you sure you didn't make that call?"

"I told you I didn't. I wouldn't call you or anyone else at that hour." He was annoyed and to prove it took a hefty bite out of the large green apple in his fist. The noise made by his strong healthy teeth sounded to her like a cement mixer.

"Stop eating, for God's sake." She blushed, not meaning to shout. Her hand went involuntarily to her throat.

"Vita, I've never seen you this way. Never heard you talk that way. What's eating you?"

"Nothing's eating me." Despite herself her tone was high-pitched.

"Well, my gosh. You're talking like you're panicking."

"I'm not panicking," she said, frightened at his words.

"Look, Vita, why don't you take a week or two off and go see your ma?" Herbert looked really concerned as he took her hand. "I mean it, girl. I've never seen you get the jumps like this."

She shook his hand off. "Stop saying that. I'm not getting any jumps. I'm—I'm maybe—well, maybe I was a little scared by that call. I mean the papers are full of horrible stories about prowlers and sex criminals." She stopped and pursed her lips. "Herbert, don't write home about this, please. Mom'll be awfully worried."

Herbert shook his head. "I wasn't going to write. I was going to call. I'm really concerned about you, Vita. I've never seen you like this, and I've known you a long time."

Vita tried to smile bravely. "It's all right. I guess I just—I mean I've been a little tired lately from too much work and driving on that freeway at rush hour. I'll just take a sleeping pill and I'll be okay in the morning. But please promise me you won't call."

"Well, I don't know, Vita," Herbert said stolidly. He took her hands in his. "Look, Vita. Why don't you let me take care of things for you."

"What things, Herbert?"

He looked embarrassed. "Well, Vita. I mean, I've known you all my life. I want to help you any way I can."

"I know, Herbert. And I'm grateful to you."

"Vita, what I mean is—Vita, I'm crazy about you. I want to marry you." His Adam's apple began to bob up and down nervously. Suddenly, clumsily, he gave her a bear hug.

Vita's eyes opened wide with surprise. "Oh no, Herbert. Not now. Not tonight. Oh please." She broke away from him.

He looked puzzled. "What's wrong with tonight? I was going to ask you tonight anyhow. I had it all planned." He removed a jeweler's case from his pocket and opened it to reveal a small engagement ring.

For a moment Vita thought she would giggle openly in his face. Then she caught herself. The impression of being caught in an unreal situation was so strong she wanted to pinch herself. There was something grotesque in being proposed to tonight when she was trying to control her growing fear that she might be the next victim of the prowler.

Herbert was staring at her, bewildered. "Is something wrong, Vita?"

44

Her strange expression alarmed him. "Are you angry or something?"

Vita kissed him quickly. "No. No. Oh, Herbert, please don't ask me now."

"But I've already asked you," Herbert answered, speaking slowly and logically. His eyes looked worried. "Vita, what on earth is wrong?"

"Nothing, nothing. Just let's not go on with this now, Herbert."

"Why not?" Herbert's pride had been hurt by her tone and she knew it. "I thought you expected this all the time. Why, your mother told me that—"

She cut him off sharply. "Please, Herbert. I'm in no condition to listen to a proposal tonight. Can't you see that?"

Her shrill tone and the trembling of her body alarmed him. He stood up and took her in his arms. He could feel her shivering against him. "For Pete's sake, Vita, you shouldn't take these stories so seriously. I've heard you say yourself they're circulation builders. There's nothing to worry about. He's too smart to double back on his tracks in the same neighborhood. He's probably out in the San Fernando Valley or out of town by now. He knows all the cops are looking for him. Now calm down, honey. Everything's going to be all right."

His authoritative tone and the immense self-assurance in his voice soothed her. After a moment, she pulled away from him and smiled.

"I guess I have been a little silly about it. It's just that I've never quite got a call like that. It was very weird—I mean his way of talking and the things he kept saying about my legs and my—everything. He sounded a little like somebody unbalanced."

"Sure. Forget it. I'll call you in the morning. You'll feel much better. And by that time there'll probably be a story that the guy's been found in Arizona or New Mexico. That's the pattern of these types. I know. They never hang around."

Vita smiled gratefully at him as they reached the door. She said nothing as he kissed her good night and started for the door, controlling her desire to call him back. She stood near the door and watched him tinker with the motor of his car, letting it idle for a minute as usual. The sound of the motor turning over matched the turbulent movements of her heart. She felt sick to her stomach as Herbert turned on the lights and slowly edged away from the curb.

8

BEHIND THE LOCKED DOOR, she felt horribly alone and isolated. She thought of taking a sleeping pill in order to sleep but dismissed the idea a second later. She did not want to be caught in a deep slumber by any sex criminal.

It was only ten o'clock. Perhaps John would call, she thought, and suggest coming over.

Suddenly, impulsively, she reached into a kitchen cupboard and removed a bottle of whisky. It was a bottle of Scotch that she had bought to give John an occasional drink when he brought her home at night. Now she felt she needed its courage. She poured herself a stiff shot and drank it straight. Its warmth suffused her instantly and reddened her cheeks. She took a second shorter drink and felt better.

She lay back on the sofa and rubbed her bare feet deliciously against the cool pillows, enjoying their smoothness. She felt better in a few moments, but a new loneliness filled her. She wished John would call or come up and talk to her. The feel of his cheek on hers came back to her, the wetness of his deep kisses, and the way he held her, the flat of his palm hard against her back, her bosom flattened against his chest. She felt her cheeks tingle and the blood rushed to her head. If John had been there now, this minute, and had wanted her, she would not have refused.

In Chicago it had been simple. Despite the heavy drinking and the dancing which had made her woozy, she had not lost her head when John took her to her room. Not even when she knew she wanted him too and that she could rationalize the whole thing by telling herself she was too drunk to care. But the old fear of sex that had been ground into her by her mother had held. Her mother had told her many times that physical intimacy was a horrible thing, and that a woman had to submit to have children. And in a rare mood of bitter confidence, she had told Vita that when she had submitted to Vita's father, she had forced herself to drink as much blackberry brandy as she could get down. She had not said any more. But the picture of her mother, getting herself drunk to endure lovemaking, had stayed with her.

46

John had been understanding about her fears. He had been tight, almost as tight as she was. And her fingers had clutched at his neck as she kissed him good night.

He had kissed her hard then, misinterpreting everything. He moved her slowly, tenderly, to the bed.

"I love you very much, darling," he had said, moving his fingers tenderly along her arm. And she had kissed him, loving him as much as she could love anyone. She felt warm and good and did not want him to leave.

"I love you," she had said and put her arms around him, as if her words might make him bolt.

Then it had happened. His hand had cupped her breast as he kissed her hard, wetly, with his breath coming too quickly in a way that raised hackles on her flesh. And his other hand had burrowed under her skirt and caressed the warm flesh of her thighs and he had put his weight on her. She had wanted to scream, but his lips stifled her. A few seconds later when he stopped kissing her, she was too terrified to make an outcry. She looked at him, her eyes distended, her cheeks burning, as he removed her clothes, pausing after taking off her dress to kiss her tenderly. The hair on the back of his hands, when it touched her bare breasts in an involuntary movement, made her shudder. And again he misinterpreted this as desire. She lay there naked and watching him remove his clothes, and smiling. And when she saw the dark hair of his chest, she fainted.

When she came to a few minutes later, he was fully dressed and she was under the covers. His eyes were almost frantic with concern. The perspiration was thick on his forehead and his lips trembled.

Afterwards she tried to explain her fears and how they bottled up whatever she felt, how they tore at the very tenderness even while it was growing. He had understood and had been very patient. And he had asked her to marry him as soon as he could get a divorce.

9

VITA UNDRESSED SLOWLY in her bedroom, spent a few moments brushing her hair and then rubbed a lotion on her face. Then she lay in bed with the small lamp on the night table burning, and stared at the ceiling. She was thinking about the play she and John were going to see next Saturday—a Broadway hit which was being done in Hollywood—when the telephone rang shrilly in the living room. She lay still, hardly breathing. The telephone continued to blast the silent darkness. Vita stole a look at her watch. It was twelve-fifteen. Who could it be? Not John. He never called her past eleven-thirty. She had asked him not to unless it was urgent. It might be Herbert, checking on her safety. But even that was unlikely. The third possibility frightened her so much she could not put it into words. It hovered in her mind like a dark shadow. She lay absolutely still, as if her most involuntary movement might betray her fear to the caller. But the telephone continued to ring maddeningly for more than five minutes.

Finally it stopped and she breathed easier. If it had been the prowler, she hoped he was convinced she was not at home. Perhaps that was how he arranged his visits. He waited until it was after midnight and if the victim was at home, he called on her. She remembered that the last attack had taken place in daylight. "Oh the devil with it," she told herself. "Sleep, sleep, sleep!" She tried to will herself to sleep. But her mind was racing now and would not stop. She put out the light and closed her eyes. She had lain there that way for perhaps ten minutes when the telephone rang again.

Vita dug her nails into the side of the bed, listening to the instrument's demanding cry. She prayed for it to stop. Then she said aloud. "I'm not home." The thought struck her that it might be John Palmer. She listened to the continued ringing. This time it couldn't be the prowler. He wouldn't ring that long so soon after his first call. It must be John, calling to find out how she was. Or perhaps Herbert. She jumped out of bed and ran into the dark living room. She picked the instrument up from its cradle, but as she put it to her ear, she felt a dull click as the other party hung up. She shuddered and put the instrument back. Either the prowler knew that she was home or it was one of those coincidences in which one person hangs up just as another picks up the telephone. She sat by the telephone for a minute, waiting. When it rang again, she jumped. It seemed so loud.

"Hello?" she said softly. There was a disturbing clicking noise and she said again, "Hello?"

"Hello," a male voice answered. Vita felt herself tremble. It was the same voice as the night before. "I thought you weren't at home. You took so long to answer."

48

Vita kept the telephone glued to her ear. She felt paralyzed.

"I was just thinking about what you must look like in that nightgown. You are dressed for bed, aren't you? I'm sure you are at this hour." The voice raced on, unconcerned with her responses.

"Funny. I was thinking this afternoon that you must look lovely in your nightgown. I said to myself, she must be really something to look at. A girl like you with such beautiful breasts and long legs and the kind of robust thighs you like to see on a woman. You know what you remind me of—I mean what your breasts and thighs remind me of. Ever see any paintings by Rubens? He liked to paint women like that. I bought me a book of his reproductions the other day and boy—those women he painted—they're so thick and juicy, why they're almost fit to eat. Well, you're like that, Vita. I don't like these skinny girls, nothing but a rag, a bone and a hank of hair—that's Shakespeare. I do lots of reading. You may not know it to look at me. Most people, they see a man like me, they think I'm dumb, illiterate. Actually I'm much better read than most people. Self-educated. Not much schooling. I hated that stupid school I was in. Couldn't wait to get out and fish. You ever fish in a good trout stream? Lots of good ones where I come from. Best thing was after I made enough money to buy a good pole, I'd just go off and fish. I liked that better than anything. And if you were real quiet, you could see some boys and girls swimming in the nude up near the old farm that burned down. One night I was hiding behind a big bush and I watched some girls swimming by moonlight and they came out with their breasts all wet and shaking and one of the men saw me and lit out after me and I hit him with a stone."

The voice stopped and in its place was a slurping sound which terrified Vita.

"You listening, Vita? Maybe you'd like me to come in for a little while. Have some tea with milk maybe? I'm very close to you."

A few seconds later the voice said querulously. "You want me to come up or are you asleep already?"

The possibility that he might come galvanized Vita into responding. "No. I'm sleeping. Please." A dim recollection of what one was supposed to do with a psychopath kept her voice even.

"You sure now, Vita? I could come by in five minutes. I'm just down the street a piece."

Vita fought to keep the fear out of her voice. "Thank you," she said evenly, "but I was just falling asleep when you called. I've been so tired all day."

"Can I come by some other time?" the voice asked petulantly. "Tomorrow? Just a little while. I won't hurt you. I just want to talk to you and see you naked. All naked. I want to look at your sunburned skin and the white part of your breasts. And I just want to touch you all over with my fingers. Just to run my fingers along the soft tender skin on the inside of your thighs. I love a woman's softness there." The voice was droning on with a curious singsong rhythm as if the speaker was hypnotizing himself by unrolling all these images. "And I want to squeeze your beautiful, round breasts and kiss them. That's all. I don't want to hurt you, Vita. And I don't want to touch you in that special place women are afraid to let men touch them. I hate that place. It's evil, it drives men to hell. It's the dwelling place of Satan. I don't want to get into that place. That's what women don't understand. They all think I want to get inside them and hurt them. But I don't want to hurt anyone. It's just that they get frightened and want to yell and tip off the cops. Then I get scared and I get a funny feeling and I have to stop them.

"I can kill a woman in a couple of minutes with my hands. I can squeeze her neck like a chicken and when I get scared my hands don't even listen to me—they squeeze the scream off. You understand me, Vita? I can't help it. I'm so confused when it happens I don't even know who I am or where. I just have to stop her from tipping off the cops. You understand?"

"Yes," Vita said hoarsely.

"The papers are all wrong, Vita. I don't visit these women to kill them or rape them. I love women. I think they're the finest creatures the Lord ever created. Just sometimes, I don't even know when, a feeling comes over me and I want to love them up, to touch them. Especially the parts they hide from men. Their breasts and their thighs and the lovely round parts behind."

Vita felt herself becoming nauseous. She wanted to hang up. But she was terrified that the act might frighten him, might make him want to kill her as he had killed the others. And he had said he was close by.

"Are you listening, Vita?" the voice asked. "I asked you if you knew Frisco?"

"Yes," she said slowly.

"Well I was saying this feeling comes over me anytime. Like it did there. I was walking down Market Street and

50

feeling a little hungry. I bought some popcorn, so I wouldn't get too hungry. Well, there was a teen-age girl in the same place I bought the popcorn. She had the loveliest behind I ever saw, so I followed her. Pretty soon a sailor came after her and tried to pick her up. I got mad. I saw her first. She was a lovely thing, tall and dark with sharp breasts just ready to jump from her jersey and a behind I was itching to get my hands on. I followed them close—but not too close. He took her to a park and laid her down on the grass. I hid behind a bush and watched him take off her panties and take her breasts out and play with her all over. And I got mad 'cause I saw her first and I wanted her. I got so excited watching this boy play with her I nearly died. I picked up a stone and I hit him on the head just as he was standing up to let his pants down and I guess I killed him. And then I jumped on the girl and felt her behind and I wouldn't have done nothing to her if she hadn't got panicky and yelled. Then my hands just throttled her." The voice went on sorrowfully. "Poor little thing. I hadn't wanted to kill her but she screamed and when I hear a girl scream I don't know what I'm doing."

Vita hung up suddenly and ran to the bathroom. She was sick before she reached the bowl. She sat on the toilet seat, paralyzed with fear. The story of the brutal murder of the sailor and his pick-up had been more than she could stand. Trembling, she went to the living room and tried the front door. It was locked. She bolted it. She tried the windows. They were unlocked. She worked furiously to turn the catches. The thing she wanted to do was to go where people were. Any people. She would go out of her mind if she remained in the house alone. She felt like a canary waiting for a hungry cat to devour it. The prowler's horrible account of his attack on the girl and her sailor friend had stimulated the secret fear she had always had of being raped.

She should not have hung up on him, she thought wildly. Now he might come to the house. He might even be there outside now, waiting to get in. She must run into the street. She ripped off the nightgown, soiled with her vomit, and ran into the bedroom. She opened the closet, hastily pulled a dress from its hanger and pulled it down over her. In her feverish hurry, she ripped the garment as she tried to pull it down over her head. She kept trying to force her head through the opening, but her nervous hands and movements succceeded only in getting the dress all tangled. She began to sob with fear and a feeling of complete helplessness

51

against an immovable force. She ripped wildly at the dress to get it off her now so she could get another.

Finally she disengaged herself. She opened the wardrobe closet and hunted for another dress. She could not see very well by the dim light of the table lamp. She started to turn the switch of the room light and stopped. If the prowler were in the neighborhood he would see the light and assume she was waiting for him. She put out the small lamp and crouched beside the bed trembling. She did not even dare go out now. He might have left wherever he telephoned from and be near the house by this time, waiting for her to open the street door.

She sat on the floor near the bed, not daring to move, and listened for any strange street sounds. She could hear nothing but the singing of some crickets outside her windows. Suddenly the tension was too much for her and she began to sob, letting out all her fear. If only John would call or come by. Or Herbert. But she knew they wouldn't. It must be at least twelve-thirty. They would be afraid of waking her up. Maybe she could call them. Or the police. The thought of having anything to do with the police disturbed her almost as much as the fear of the prowler. But at least she would be safe. No, first try to get John or Herbert. Maybe they could come and spend the night there. The idea of having either one of them spend the night in her house alone with her suddenly seemed the best solution. She didn't care, at this moment, whether it was proper or not. She knew only that she was terrified and wanted someone around. Maybe she should call Claire or Alice? She dismissed the thought. She would feel safer with a man. She would call John or Herbert. If they were both out or did not answer, she would call the police.

Suddenly her thoughts were jolted by the telephone's loud wail. She remained crouched by the bed, not daring to move, listening to it ring. What would happen if she did not answer? Would he give up for the evening or come by the house. If he were in the neighborhood, he probably was keeping her under surveillance. He knew she was still at home alone. She could not take the chance that he might get angry and come in person. Slowly she made her way to the telephone and picked up the instrument.

"Hello?" she said quietly, as emotionlessly as possible. She had to pretend nothing had happened. That they had been cut off. "I'm sorry. We were cut off."

"Oh." The voice seemed relieved. "I wondered what had happened. I thought you were mad at me or something.

Somebody had to use the booth so I waited a while. You're not mad, are you? Some girls get mad because I talk about making love and girl's bodies. You're not mad are you, Vita?"

The voice was very apologetic, anxious not to offend her in any way.

"No, no," Vita said quickly. "I'm not."

"Oh, I'm so glad. I met a woman once on a street in Gardenia. I followed her. It was dark and it was, oh around one o'clock, and I talked to her. She was a little fat, about thirty, but a nice woman. You know Gardenia?"

"Yes."

"Well, this woman. She was a little drunk I guess. Had been playing in one of them poker parlors they have up there. And she let me walk her home. Told me she had won forty-eight dollars and seventy cents. So I walk her home and we go in and she says that she's feeling good and I'm a nice-looking young guy and she's admiring my ring. So we sit down, and she says not to make any noise. She's a widow with two kids and they're sleeping inside in another room, see. Well, she gives me a drink of whisky, you know, and I kiss her and she don't mind none. Likes it even. But then I wanted her to take her clothes off and she giggles and says no. She's a mother and doesn't do things like that with strangers and especially not with her two young kids just in another room down the hall. So I say well just let me open your dress and I tell her my theories about girl's breasts and how I like to compare them and I want her to lift up her skirt so I can see if I like her legs and I tell her about how I like to measure such things. I carry a tape measure you see and I like to do that. So she starts looking at me funny. And when I push her back, very gently you understand, on this couch and pull up her skirt she gets panicky like. And I guess I got nervous, and I ripped the buttons off her dress and next thing she starts to yell and I clamped a hand over her mouth and I had to choke her a little. I didn't mean to kill her. Swear to God I didn't. I didn't even want to get inside her. I just wanted to look, Vita. You believe me, don't you?"

The voice pleaded with her to understand. "All I wanted was to touch her breasts and legs. They, never understand that. They get scared and they think I'm trying to commit rape and they start yelling, blabbing their heads off to the whole Goddamned neighborhood and I get nervous. But you believe me, don't you, Vita? Don't you? Please say you understand. It's terribly important to me."

"I understand."

"And you don't hate me?"

"No."

"If I came up later for instance and wanted you to open your dress so I could caress your breasts and run my hands under your skirt, you wouldn't get panicky?"

"No." Vita prayed for self-control. If her voice betrayed anything, it might be too late to stop him. Please God, she thought, don't let him come.

"You don't think I'm bad? You don't believe all those stories?"

"No." Vita tried. to breathe more slowly, afraid her tortured breathing might be heard over the telephone, frightening him into thinking she knew who he was and might give him away.

"Oh, that makes me glad, Vita. Vita, I love you. I think you're the most wonderful girl I ever met. Why can't I just come up for say, half an hour and have some tea with milk? I won't keep you up too late."

"Oh, please not tonight. I'm so tired and I have to be at work so early."

"Well, I thought you liked me, Vita." The voice seemed disappointed.

"I do."

"Well, how about tomorrow?"

"Yes," she said quickly, too quickly.

There was a long silence. She wanted to bite her tongue for having answered so quickly.

"You really want me to come tomorrow?" The voice sounded disbelieving.

"Yes. Yes. Tomorrow will be fine."

"What time?"

"Any time."

"How about ten-thirty or eleven?" the voice asked cagily.

"That's all right."

The voice seemed sad but resigned. "Okay, Vita. Tomorrow it is. Good-by."

He hung up without another word. She kept the instrument in her hand for a full minute after he stopped talking, unable to believe he had gone. Then she put the instrument down. She went to the window, standing near its edge, and looked outside. She could see no one pass down the dark street, which like many Los Angeles streets had too few street lights. Could she depend on his not coming tonight, she wondered. She was too frightened. Feeling as if she were in a nightmare, she watched carefully through the dark window. Far off in the distance, a dimly silhouetted figure seemed to be moving behind a rose bush. Was it a human being or just the movement of the plant in the soft evening breeze? She looked in another direction and it seemed to her that another figure was moving.

"Don't get hysterical," she said out loud to herself. "Don't for God's sake get hysterical." There was probably nothing out there—nobody at all. But as she looked she could not be sure.

She moved back to the telephone and quickly dialed John's number. It was one o'clock. He should be home by now. She heard the instrument ring at the other end, but no one answered. Oh, John, she thought, please pick up the phone!

She let the telephone ring for several minutes. John's failure to answer was maddening. Why wasn't he home when she needed him? She replaced the instrument, lifted it quickly and dialed Herbert's number. He answered immediately.

"Herbert!" she cried with relief. "Herbert! Please come here."

"Vita? For Pete's sakes, what's happened?" He sounded alarmed. "Someone try to break in? Are you all right?"

"Herbert, I—I can't talk. Please come now."

"Right. Now look. Don't get hysterical, honey. Just calm down. Keep your door locked. I'll call your name when I get there. Don't open for anyone but me." He hung up quickly.

Vita sat on the sofa until he came. She turned up the lights full, even the small table lamps and turned on the television set, to ease her tension. She was so terrified that she was not sure she recognized Herbert's voice yelling her name until he had called for the fifth time. Finally she opened the door and looked outside. It was Herbert. The tail of his shirt hung over his trousers. Beside him was Mrs. McNulty, Vita's neighbor from across the street.

"I heard this young man screaming your name," she began apologetically, and I wanted to call the police. You know there's a prowler loose. What was all that screaming about before?"

Vita put her arms around Herbert and said nothing. She was relieved to see him there and had hardly noticed Mrs. McNulty.

"It's after one o'clock," Mrs. McNulty said.

Herbert suddenly blushed. He let Vita go and tucked in his shirt.

"I'm sorry I woke you. Miss Reynolds had—well, she was sick and it looked like an emergency. So I—" He looked helplessly at Vita.

Mrs. McNulty, a fat woman in her fifties, brushed her gray hair back and stared doubtfully at Vita. "What's the matter with you? If you were sick, you should have called me. What's wrong?"

Vita was too exhausted to lie. "I just got a phone call from a man who sounded like the prowler. He said he was in the neighborhood and wanted to come over. I was scared to death."

Mrs. McNulty looked worried. "In the neighborhood? How do you know?"

"He told me," Vita said, closing her eyes. "He said he wanted to do things to me. He said he killed a woman in Gardenia because she wanted to call the police. I was so terrified I couldn't step out that door."

"Are you going to call the police?" Mrs. McNulty asked suddenly.

Vita looked uncertain. "I suppose I should."

Herbert scowled. "Wait a minute." He led them inside the house and they sat in the living room. "You call the police, you're going to have this all over town. In the papers. Do you want that?"

Vita was still too shocked to think. "I don't know, Herbert."

"It may give them a clue to catch him," Mrs. McNulty put in. "You can't just keep a thing like this to yourself."

Herbert ignored her. "Vita, if the police get this, they'll be all over the place asking questions. The story will get in all the papers, even in Iowa."

Vita stared at him, suddenly aware of what he meant. "No. No. It would be terrible for Mother." She turned to Mrs. McNulty. "My mother's very high-strung and she's got a heart condition."

Mrs. McNulty looked sympathetic. "That's too bad. No I guess it would be dangerous for her to read anything like that." She pursed her lips and thought for a minute. Then she brightened. "Wait a minute. I'm sure if you asked the police they wouldn't give your name to the press."

Herbert looked unconvinced. "I don't know."

Mrs. McNulty spoke to Vita. "You have to tell them what happened. You've been reading those stories. The only way the police can get the man is to follow up every attempt, to check everything he says or does. My daughter is a secretary

56

in a law firm. I know that's how they work in an investigation. And I know you can help them."

"But he made no attempt," Herbert said.

"Yes, but he talked to her about that killing in Gardenia. I read about it two weeks ago. He must have told her something they can check on."

Vita nodded wearily. "She's right. He told me a lot of things."

"You've got to call them, honey. I know it's not a pleasant experience to get involved with the police. But I'm sure they'll respect your wishes as far as your name is concerned. You have to let them know. My God, you don't know where this maniac may turn up next. How would you feel if he raped or killed somebody down the street and you knew you could have stopped him. You don't want that on your conscience. I'm sure you don't."

Herbert said nothing. Vita seemed unable to make up her mind, then she said wearily, "She's right. I'll have to tell them."

"I'll talk to them," Herbert said quickly. "You just sit down and relax." He went to the telephone and called the Hollywood police precinct.

10

SLOWLY, PAINSTAKINGLY, Herbert told the police sergeant who answered the telephone that the prowler had called Vita and had threatened to come in person. He suggested they send a detective around to get the full details.

He could hear the police sergeant speaking to someone else. Then another voice came on the telephone and asked to speak to Vita.

The detective spoke to her for several minutes, asking her questions about what the man had said and how he had sounded. Then he hung up. Half an hour later, a man who identified himself as Lieutenant Goldberg called and said he was coming immediately. He arrived twenty minutes later.

Vita found herself speaking to a small, plump man, about five-feet-five, with a kind face and soft brown eyes. The detective was semi-bald and he seemed very tired except for his

57

eyes, which were very alert. He grew tense when she told her story. He listened carefully while his companion, a plainclothesman, took notes.

"I'm sorry to bother you people so late," he said sitting down next to her. "My name is Goldberg. Lieutenant Goldberg. And this is Sergeant Farley. We've been working on the prowler case for several weeks. Mind if I just shoot ahead?"

Vita nodded, liking the man. He had a matter-of-fact honesty that made things easy.

"Okay. Now tell me everything that happened. From the very beginning. Leave nothing out. I mean, if he said anything embarrassing—you can write it on this pad. These characters say things over the phone that would make even me blush.

"Don't withhold anything, though. Everything he said may be significant and lead to something." He stopped and looked at Farley. "I'd better call and see whether Jenkins has heard anything. Those boys who went on patrol around here may have heard something or seen him."

He called his station and spoke to the desk sergeant for a moment. There was nothing and he hung up. For the next few minutes he listened carefully to Vita. Several times he made her go back and repeat several things. Finally he stood up and sighed.

"Okay. That's it. It sounds like it could be him. But—" He looked steadily at the girl. "Tell me, miss. I mean, don't resent this. I've got to know. Did you ever have any psychiatric treatment? I mean ever suffer from any mental ailments?"

"I don't think you have any right to say that to her," Herbert said stoutly. Vita smiled. Herbert liked to be gallant at the wrong time. Mrs. McNulty, who had been watching quietly, gave him a dirty look.

Goldberg regarded him coldly. "Look, sonny. This is a job, and these are questions I have to ask."

"Don't mind the questions, miss," Farley said in his soft voice. "Lieutenant Goldberg don't mean no harm. He's just got to be sure, that's all."

"Of course," Vita said. "Can I get you both some coffee?"

Goldberg smiled. "Thanks." He walked to the window and looked out for a minute. "I can't figure why Los Angeles gets so many of these lunkheads. In New York they slit your throat, but you don't have peepers or creeps who go around jumping lonely women." Mrs. McNulty looked very shocked.

"The statistics show otherwise, Lieutenant, if you'll pardon the correction," Farley noted. "For instance, take 1956. You know how many sex crimes were committed in the five boroughs of New York?"

Goldberg glared at him. "Okay, okay. Forget it. A guy can't open his mouth here without one of you native boosters hopping into it. I'm sorry. California is paradise on wheels. Maybe the statistics tell otherwise. But in the ten years I wore a New York badge, I didn't see so many varied methods of indecent behavior as I have here. Guys who expose themselves to little girls, jokers who walk along freeway exits waiting for women to stall in their cars, guys who print their initials on girls' thighs with cigar butts."

Suddenly he saw Vita coming back from the kitchen and stopped.

"Coffee'll be ready in a minute, Lieutenant," Vita said. The police officer's authoritative personality made her feel easier. She had calmed down a great deal.

Mrs. McNulty got up reluctantly. "Well I guess I can go back now. I'd like to stay. But my kids'll be worried."

Vita smiled warmly. "Won't you stay and have some coffee, Mrs. McNulty? It's perking."

The Irishwoman pushed back her unruly hair and shook her head. "No, thanks. I won't get to sleep at all if I have any coffee at this hour. You just calm down, miss. Don't let yourself get nervous about this." She left still shaking her head and staring at Goldberg.

"You'll stay won't you, Herbert?" Vita asked.

Herbert smiled. "All night if I have to. I don't have to be at school until eight-thirty." He looked at Goldberg as if daring him to say no. They stopped talking for a few minutes while Vita served them coffee and some cake. While he ate, Goldberg kept making notes in a leather notebook he carried.

"Look, Miss Reynolds. I wrote down a few things this boy said on the phone. He didn't give away much. But a few things I noted. Let me check them with you. First, this guy sounded like a young man, right?"

Vita thought for a minute. "I think so. I mean it's not always easy to tell. But there was a young quality about his voice. And it seemed to have some Middle-Western thing about it—like voices I remembered from back home. You know." She looked at Herbert and reddened. "For a minute I even thought it might be Mr. Buhler or John Palmer playing a practical joke."

Goldberg looked at her. "Who's this John Palmer?"

"I could imagine that character pulling something like this as a joke. It's right down his Madison Avenue alley," Herbert said scornfully.

"Herbert, you have no right to say anything like that. John wouldn't do anything like this in a hundred years. And you know that."

Goldberg waited impatiently. "All right, so he wouldn't do anything like this in a hundred years. Who is he?"

"He's a friend of mine," Vita began slowly.

"You go out with him a lot?"

Herbert curled his lip at this, and Goldberg could not ignore it.

"You don't like this guy, huh?" he asked Herbert.

"Frankly, no."

"What makes you think he might do anything like this?"

"Oh I didn't say he did do it," Herbert said quickly. "I'm not accusing him. I just meant it isn't beyond him. That's all."

"Lieutenant, this is crazy. I know it wasn't John. I know John's voice. And I talked to him. I was worried at first because the man who called spoke about my bathing suit and certain birthmarks which—" She reddened.

"Go on," said Goldberg kindly. "All this may be helpful. Don't be shy. Or would you rather tell me privately," he added, looking at Herbert.

"No—no," Vita said. "I'm just a little mixed up. You see, I took some pictures at the beach with Mr. Palmer."

"What beach?"

Vita looked very embarrassed. "Is that important, Lieutenant?"

"Certainly. The prowler may have seen you there."

"Well, it was at San Clemente, between Laguna Beach and San Diego."

Herbert looked incredulous. "You went down to San Clemente with Palmer?"

Goldberg said, "How long were you there?"

Vita dug her fist hard into the sofa pillows. "I don't see how that has anything to do with this, Lieutenant."

Goldberg closed his eyes in infinite patience about women's strange mental processes. "Look, let me be the detective, miss. It's important. It may lead to one bit of information which we can use to track him down. One person who may have seen him there. Now please, please don't be coy."

Herbert shook his head unbelievingly. "You went away with a married man for a whole weekend?"

Vita looked frightened. "It wasn't like that, Herbert. We had separate rooms in a motel."

Herbert still looked astonished. "I'd never have thought this possible. Not you, Vita."

Goldberg glared at Buhler. "Look, sonny, mind your own business. We're not checking into the young lady's morals here. We're trying to find a dangerous criminal, a murderer. Now if you can't shut up, get out. There isn't any reason for you to hang around anyhow." He looked at Vita. "Want me to send Mr. Righteous Indignation home, miss?"

"Never mind," Herbert said with injured pride. "I'm going. I don't want to hear any more of this."

Vita looked worriedly at him as he started for the door. "I still think you ought to check this Palmer's story," Herbert said. "It's funny this mysterious caller knew all about her beach party."

Vita was furious. "That's stupid, Herbert. What possible motive could John have for such a thing?"

"How do I know? Maybe he's trying to scare you off. He's a married man and maybe you're getting to be a problem? How can anybody tell what goes on in anybody's mind. Some of the things my own school kids think of scare me."

"I think you're just jealous and out of your mind. I think you'd better leave right now," Vita shot back.

"Look, Vita, I didn't mean to hurt you," Herbert said.

"Please get out of here," Vita wailed, unable to look at him. "Get out. I don't want to hear any more of these accusations."

"Vita," Herbert began. "I only meant—"

"Look, sonny, the lady says go. So go." Goldberg had listened wearily to the scene and felt a little sorry for Buhler. The boy obviously had a bad case on the girl and she didn't even know he was alive. But he had his own work to do, and it was the middle of the night. He had no time, or stomach, for lovers' quarrels.

11

BEFORE HERBERT COULD ANSWER Lieutenant Goldberg, the doorbell rang sharply. Instantly everyone in the room stopped talking and waited. Vita felt a shudder run through her, an involuntary trembling that made her knees feel like jelly. For a few seconds she stopped breathing, almost as if doing so might warn the newcomer. The ringing continued at short intervals. Goldberg motioned to them both to remain silent and where they were. His gestures frightened Vita more than the sound of the doorbell. Goldberg silently ordered Farley to go out through the kitchen exit.

The police officer was convinced this was the prowler. She could tell by every gesture, every careful move he made. Buhler watched Goldberg with a curious fascination as he slowly took a gun from a shoulder holster, waved quickly at them to get into the bedroom and took his place silently behind the door. For a moment Vita was too paralyzed to move. The whole scene seemed so unreal. The detective was standing near the door, waiting for the newcomer to enter, or perhaps for Farley to overcome him.

Goldberg threw them an impatient glance and this, more than anything else, sent them back. From the corner of the bedroom, Vita and Herbert stared at the detective as he waited. The bell rang once more and then they heard a key turning in the door. Goldberg flattened himself against the wall near the door and waited. The sight of the small, balding detective holding a gun in the brightly lit living room made the scene very unreal to Vita. She felt for a few seconds as if she had been watching a cops and robbers program on the television set and that the characters had resumed their scene by stepping out of her set and onto her living room carpet. None of it seemed to be true. Neither the taut figure of the watchful detective, holding a gun in his right hand, the sight of Herbert Buhler's transfixed stare as his steely gray eyes looked at the door, or the sound of the key.

Whoever was trying to unlock the door was having trouble. He was obviously trying to use a skeleton key, unless— Vita suddenly reddened as a new idea came into her head. John had a key to the apartment! The last thing she wanted now was to have him come in like this. She moved forward and felt Herbert grip her wrist in a strong, quick movement. Then it was too late. The door swung open and John Palmer came in. A second later, Goldberg had leaped behind him and dug his gun into his back. "Okay, put them up and keep them there," Goldberg said in a corrosive voice. "Fast."

Farley came in quickly and stood respectfully by his superior's side. "I've been watching him for five minutes," he said. "I was all set to drop him if he made a break." Farley put his gun back into his holster.

The look on Palmer's face was almost comic. He stared at the two police officers, trying to figure the whole thing out. Then he saw Vita and Buhler standing in the entrance to the bedroom. For a moment he was speechless. The hardness of the gun barrel against his back· was so terrifying he could only stare helplessly ahead of him.

"All right," Goldberg said suddenly. "Put the cuffs on him. Farley jumped forward and handcuffed Palmer in a few seconds, working deftly and professionally. Then suddenly everybody found their voices at once.

"Wait a minute," Palmer said, protesting loudly. "What the hell do you think you're doing?" Farley ignored him.

"Lieutenant, this is Mr. Palmer," Vita shouted as Farley put the handcuffs on.

Goldberg looked funny. "*Palmer?* You mean the guy we just talked about?"

"Yes," Vita shouted. "Please take those things off."

"Ask him what's he doing here," Herbert said maliciously. "How does he happen to wander in here at three in the morning—and using a key?"

Goldberg threw Buhler an annoyed glance. But the question was sound. He looked at Palmer expectantly. The young advertising executive stood there in his dark, pin-striped suit and stared grimly at Buhler. He remained silent.

"You heard the question, Mr. Palmer," Goldberg said politely.

Palmer looked at Goldberg as if he wanted to speak, then glanced quickly at Vita and Buhler. Vita stared back at him with what seemed to be a mute appeal in her eyes. Buhler was smiling knowingly, like a smug cat who had just swallowed a mouse. The arrogance of his expression made John Palmer want to strangle him.

"I said what are you doing here," Goldberg repeated. "You want to tell me here, or do you want to tell me down at the station house?"

Buhler laughed nervously. "You've got him over a barrel, Lieutenant."

"I—I found the key under a doormat outside," Palmer said suddenly. "I kept ringing and there was no answer and I was worried about Miss Reynolds."

Farley started to interrupt, but Goldberg eyed him quickly and he stopped.

"What were you worried about?" Goldberg said, watching him carefully.

"I knew this prowler was roaming the neighborhood and I

was worried. And I knew she was very upset about that call last night. I was at a dinner party out in Pasadena and couldn't call her until late."

Vita looked at him gratefully. "You did call, then?"

"Yes, around midnight, I think," John said. "Nobody answered. Then I tried again later and the line was busy. I tried every few minutes and the line was still tied up. I began to worry about the line being tied up. I knew no friend of hers would start a long conversation at that hour. So I decided to come over. I knew I couldn't sleep. I got dressed and came over."

"What took you so long?" Buhler asked disbelievingly.

"I live over near Arcadia," John said angrily, "and I had to stop for gas." He stared at Buhler with distaste. "It may not register on your little provincial brain, but this is exactly the kind of scene I was trying to avoid."

"What do you mean?" Goldberg said. "What scene? You thought Buhler might be with her, you mean?"

"No. This is a quiet residential neighborhood, Lieutenant and Vita—Miss Reynolds—is anxious to avoid any talk that might get back to her mother. Naturally I hesitated a long time before coming down. I knew it might look funny to have a man call on her at this hour. That's why I waited so long. I kept trying to reach her by phone from my home for a while. Then I got undressed and went to bed. Only I couldn't sleep. The prowler story had scared me too. After a while I decided maybe she was too scared to even answer the telephone and I didn't try again. I didn't want to scare the girl to death. I was also afraid the prowler might be here and had taken the phone off the hook."

"Ask him if he always goes around putting keys in peoples' doors when they don't answer doorbells," Herbert said sneering.

"Goddamn you, shut up or I'll bash that stupid face of yours in," Palmer said angrily. "I've had just about enough of the smug, small-town indignation of yours." He stepped toward Buhler menacingly.

"I'm not afraid of you," Buhler retorted. "Any time you want to meet me anywhere, I'll be glad to accommodate you."

"I'm warning you, Buhler," Palmer said quietly as Goldberg watched them, making no move to interrupt. "I've stayed away from you only because Vita's been afraid you'd blab to her mother and I didn't want the old woman coming down with another heart attack. But I've wanted to give you a dusting over ever since you appointed yourself her guardian angel. Spying on everything she does, everybody she sees, blackmailing her into going out with you, out of fear you're going to upset the applecart."

"I didn't blackmail anybody," Buhler said, reddening. "You've got her hypnotized or something and she's fallen for you. But down deep she knows it's wrong to take up with a married man and she needs somebody who's decent and believes in the church."

"Stop it, stop it, both of you," Vita shouted. "Stop them, Lieutenant, please."

Goldberg moved quickly to Palmer's side and took his arm in a firm but friendly way. "Okay, buddy. You've made your point. Now, is there anyone who saw you in Arcadia an hour ago?"

Vita's eyes widened in amazement. "Oh, no! You're not trying to say John is the man? It's the most idiotic thing I ever heard."

The little detective eyed her philosophically. "Did I say he was, miss? How do I know who the prowler is? But anyone who turns up in a sleeping neighborhood at four o'clock in the morning—I don't automatically assume he's dropping in for tea."

"But I know this man," Vita protested. "He works in my office. He couldn't do anything like that. Not in a million years."

"Don't believe her," Buhler cut in impatiently. "He's a married man and he's probably been doing the whole thing to scare her. I know his type. They get some poor girl to go haywire just for kicks. Then when their wives kick up a fuss, they have to knock it off."

He wanted to say more, but he was cut down by a swift uppercut to the jaw by the handcuffed fists of John Palmer. Herbert looked a little bewildered and went down like a deflated tire. As he did, Farley leaped to pick him up. Goldberg pushed Palmer to the couch and sat him down forcibly.

"You stay put, Joe Louis, or I'll have you in a police car so fast it'll make your head swim." He waited until Herbert had come to and was fingering his jaw, staring balefully at John. Vita looked as if she were trying to keep from crying. She let Farley move her gently to the armchair near the couch.

"Now look, both of you," Goldberg said finally. "I didn't come out here in the middle of the night to watch a third-rate television comedy. And I didn't bargain for any of

65

this Romeo and Juliet crap. A murder's been committed in the neighborhood. Others have been committed in different parts of Hollywood. Whoever it is is an unbalanced killer. He might be trying to kill or rape someone right now, while you people are playing your little soap opera. I am not accusing anybody here of being the killer, or even the guy who phoned Miss Reynolds. But I can't afford to leave anything unquestioned. Is that clear?

"Now, after this, you can either give me some specific answers in plain English to questions I ask, or we can all go down to the station house and do it there. Now how do you want it?"

Before they could answer, the telephone rang. There was a sudden hushed silence. No one moved. Goldberg motioned silently to Vita to pick up the instrument. She shook her head, trembling. He scowled at her and nodded to the phone. "Pick it up, will you?"

"I—I can't. I wouldn't be able to control my voice," she said nervously.

"Please, answer it, Miss Reynolds," Goldberg said quietly. "Take a deep breath and do it slowly. Say each word slowly, carefully, as if you were throwing stones into a lake. He won't notice anything. But he may just possibly give us a clue to where he is. And he may be coming over here."

"Leave her alone," Palmer said angrily. "Can't you see she's close to collapsing, for God's sake."

Goldberg turned to him and narrowed his eyes. "If I were you, Romeo, I'd shut my face. This may be the best thing that ever happened, as far as you're concerned."

"Just what does that mean?" John asked. The telephone continued to ring, like some background music written especially for the tense scene.

"If it is the prowler, it'll prove that nice, romantic story you told us a minute ago. Catch?" He turned to Vita. "Now look, for the last time, answer it. He's not going to keep ringing all night."

Vita moved slowly to the telephone, but before she reached it, it stopped ringing. When she picked it up she heard only the faint buzz of a dead line.

"I'm terribly sorry," Vita said and sat down heavily in her chair. "I'm terribly sorry."

Goldberg looked at the floor and said nothing for a moment. "Okay. Okay," he said. "I guess you've had too much. We probably lost him. I think we can call it a night. We'll hang around for a few minutes in case he calls back."

Palmer raised his hands, still in the handcuffs. "What about me?"

Goldberg looked at him. "What about you, sweetheart? Oh, I'd love to book you. That's what about you. But I won't. Maybe I ought to have my head examined. Maybe it's this California climate. But I'll let you go. You may be telling the truth."

"He is," Vita said wearily. "John came here because he was worried about me. I could have proved it, if I answered the call. But I've had so much, tonight, so much. I just couldn't."

Buhler got up from the couch and wiped her perspiring forehead with a clean handkerchief. "Please, Lieutenant. She's really in bad shape."

"Okay," Goldberg said. "Better call a doctor. She looks like she might be getting close to hysteria. Turn Romeo loose, Farley."

The big sergeant unlocked the handcuffs quickly, leaving a scowling Palmer to rub his chafed wrists gingerly.

"I ought to complain to the district attorney about this treatment," he said darkly. "Maybe I will."

Goldberg shrugged. "Sticks and stones will break my bones. So complain. A guy walks into a strange house with his own key at four in the morning, and I'm supposed to treat him like Winston Churchill, I suppose."

He paused to scrutinize John carefully. "There are a lot of questions I'd like to ask you. About that key, among other things."

"That key has nothing to do with this," John retorted, rubbing his wrists, "unless you're going to believe all that baloney that hayseed spit out."

Buhler flushed and moved forward, but was restrained by Farley.

"I'll be the judge of that," the detective said. "But I'll wait till I see you tomorrow. I want to find out if the patrols have spotted anyone. I think the lady's had enough for tonight."

Vita looked alarmed. "You're not all going and leaving me here by myself?"

Goldberg smiled. "Of course not. Farley'll be here. And your friend can stay until the doctor comes, if you want him to."

Vita nodded. The telephone rang again. Everyone stared at her. She trembled and picked it up. It was the police calling Goldberg. He spoke for a few minutes and hung up. "That last call was for me. It wasn't the prowler. He probably knows we're here."

A little later two brawny uniformed cops entered and talked to Goldberg. Meanwhile Herbert called the doctor. A second siren wailed outside and she heard the brakes of a car. The phone rang twice with calls for Lieutenant Goldberg.

"Okay, we can leave now," Goldberg said finally. "I'll talk to you in your office tomorrow, Palmer. About ten."

John looked acutely embarrassed. "Can't I come and see you, Lieutenant? And also I'd appreciate it if we could keep this from the papers."

Herbert laughed unpleasantly. "He doesn't want his wife to know."

Before he could finish, John had leaped at him and hit him twice, staggering him with a left hook to his chin. Herbert recovered and rushed at John. The two men grappled as the police tried to pull them apart.

"Stop it," Vita screamed hysterically, "stop it! stop it! I can't stand anymore." She continued to scream at them to stop. Suddenly she began sobbing violently and quivered from head to foot. A second later she slumped to the floor. John and Herbert stopped grappling and stared at her.

Goldberg picked Vita up gently and carried her into the bedroom. A moment later Officer Farley was rubbing her face with witch hazel and offering her a glass of cool water. She looked up and saw a ring of worried faces: Goldberg's, Farley's, Buhler's and Palmer's. Goldberg said softly, "You just rest, honey. We're getting out of here—all except Farley. The doctor'll be along." He looked at Palmer. "As for you, buddy. You really asked for it. I'm booking you for assault."

"No," Vita cried. "Please don't arrest him. He just lost his head, Lieutenant. Please!" Her brown eyes appealed to him.

Goldberg shook his head wearily. "I'm sorry, honey. In the movies the handsome boy friend socks his rival and everybody grins. Not in my bailiwick. This is the second time your boy's got out of hand. Come on, Palmer."

Goldberg turned on his heel and moved out of the room, clutching Palmer's elbow with a tight grip. "Stay with it, Farley. 'Bye, Mr. Buhler. I may talk to you tomorrow." He was out of the room before Vita could say anything else. The sight of John being pushed from the room like a thief was so incredible she could barely believe it. She tried to pick herself up, but Farley stopped her with a gentle hand.

"Lie down, miss," he advised. "It won't do any good. The lieutenant, he's a stubborn man. And people who use their fists rile him up."

"But they can't arrest him," Vita said, startled by the shrill sound of her voice. "They can't. It'll be terrible for him. He won't be able to face anyone at the office."

. "He shouldn't have done that." Farley lit a cigarette. "Now lie still and don't make yourself any more aggravated."

"But you've got to stop them, officer. If they arrest him, he may lose his job." Vita sat up quickly and clutched at Farley's shoulder. "Please, officer, please bring them back. He can explain everything. A thing like this can ruin him. Please try to understand."

12

The doctor, a sour-looking, gray-haired man in a crumpled bankers'-gray suit gave Vita an injection and promised to look in on her again in the morning.

Farley saw the doctor to the door silently. At the entrance, the doctor smiled wanly. "That girl's been through a wringer. If there's no improvement tomorrow, we'll have to put her in the hospital."

After her daughters had gone to bed, Mrs. McNulty sat up and wondered about Vita. She also wondered about Herbert Buhler, whom Joan had accused of making improper advances toward Carlotta Green. Mrs. McNulty re-read the evening paper. In a small box near the story, there was a plea that readers should call the city desk if they received a call from anyone they suspected was the prowler. A reward of twenty-five dollars was offered for each legitimate tip. She was debating whether a tip about the goings-on across the road would get her the twenty-five dollars when Harvey Saxon took the matter out of her hands.

Saxon, who was working on the all-night shift, called Vita's house as soon as his contact at the police station told him of the latest prowler scare. Goldberg had already left, so he spoke to Farley. The Irishman, always cautious with the press, had told him the bare facts, including Mrs. McNulty's visit. A sixth sense told him that Mrs. McNulty might be in a position to supply colorful details glossed over by the detective. Actually it was just routine news work and he never expected to hit the jackpot he did. After he had assured Mrs. McNulty the twenty-five dollars was hers, he could not shut her up.

"Wait a minute," Saxon said, his voice charged with excitement. "Let me get this down. Tell me everything."

She complied gladly, full of a mother's righteous indignation. By the time she finished, he knew all about Vita, her mother, the Johnsons upstairs, Vita's habits of seeing men at three in the morning and Herbert Buhler's penchant for taking his fifteen-year-old pupils home after school. She also mentioned in passing that she had seen Walter Johnson, Vita's landlord, sneaking in and out of his own house after midnight on several occasions during the past two weeks, including tonight.

"He was there tonight?" Saxon asked encouragingly.

"Oh yes, I never sleep till late. He was coming out of his house after one A.M. and he never shows a light when he goes up there either. Very funny if you asked me. He's supposed to be making a picture up north. What's he hiding for?

The reporter whistled after she hung up. He decided to keep the nocturnal habits of Mr. Johnson to himself for the time being. There might be an interesting angle there for later development.

Half an hour later, Saxon called Goldberg at the office. "Look, Lieutenant, is this Reynolds girl a call girl or isn't she?" he asked. "If she is, it certainly adds a new twist. Call girl gets called by prowler."

"Who gave you that crap?" Goldberg asked testily.

"Never mind. Is she or not? Of course if you just want to clam up on me, go ahead. You've been blocking me on this all week anyway."

"Harvey, for Christ's sake—she's just a nice kid from the corn belt. These guys weren't laying her. They're suitors. They were both nuts about her, anxious to marry her and they locked horns. They acted like they wanted to fight a duel for her hand. Real B-movie stuff."

"Okay," Saxon said wearily. "Give me all the dope on the romance and the fight and booking the guy and we'll skip the call girl thing till you check it. This is a family newspaper anyhow."

"For Christ sakes," Goldberg said suddenly furious. "Why don't you let her alone. Let her live. She's never done anything to you."

70

"I've got to live too," Saxon shot back angrily. "You think I like being stuck on this Goddamned graveyard trick. Goddamn it, if a reporter tries to do his job honestly, you guys always accuse him of being a moral leper. Well, I'm damn sick and tired of it. This girl got her ass caught right in the middle of one of the most exciting news stories of the year. I'm sorry if it's going to hurt her feelings, but that's the way it is."

Goldberg swore under his breath and gave Saxon all the facts. When he finished Saxon laughed happily. "Christ, what a story! It's got everything. The prowler, call girls, a schoolteacher who likes jailbait and two Romeos fighting for Juliet with Lieutenant Goldberg as referee." He was deliberately corning it up for Goldberg's benefit.

"What's this about the schoolteacher?" Goldberg asked.

Saxon gleefully repeated everything Mrs. McNulty had told him about Herbert Buhler and his pupils.

"Look, please don't use that call girl angle, Harvey," Goldberg said.

The reporter laughed. "Don't worry. I couldn't have anyway. I'm not bargaining for any libel suit just because some old windbag doesn't like her neighbors."

When he had finished with Goldberg, Saxon looked up Herbert Buhler's number in the telephone book.

"Hello, Mr. Buhler?"

"Yes." Herbert's voice was sharp and cold.

"This is Harvey Saxon of the *Chronicle*. I've got some questions I'd like to ask. Now you needn't answer them, but there's quite a story about what happened tonight, and as a schoolteacher, you'll probably want to get your part of it straight."

It was an old trick he had learned in Chicago. If you ran your words close together, the other person had to listen. If you could interest him in the self-preservation idea quickly enough, he wouldn't hang up and he might just start talking.

"I've nothing to say," Herbert said slowly when Saxon had finished.

"What sort of work does Miss Reynolds do?" Saxon asked.

"Well I think you'd better talk to somebody in her office about that," Herbert said cautiously.

"Well can you give me a number I can call?" Saxon asked.

"I'd rather not," Herbert said.

"Look, Mr. Buhler, I'd like to be as helpful to you as possible—that's why I asked for your version. Surely you can

71

give me just the number. I won't tell anyone you gave it to me."

Herbert looked up Claire Bronson's number and gave it to him.

"Mr. Saxon," Herbert said in an awkward voice, "please leave my name out of the story, will you?"

"I wish I could, fella," Saxon said regretfully, "but I don't see how. You're right in the middle of it. It's not so bad. Just another fight."

"Please, Mr. Saxon," Herbert pleaded frantically, "you don't understand. I'm not only a teacher at Hollywood High. I'm a Sunday School teacher. I teach a Bible class and I'm very active in church things. This thing could not only cost me my job—it could ruin everything else. Please try to understand."

Saxon hesitated. "I'm sorry, fella," he said sincerely. "I appreciate your problem. But you can't suppress news." He hung up, looked at his typewriter for a moment and shrugged.

A few seconds later he dialed Claire Bronson's number. Claire was annoyed at being roused at four A.M. but she listened excitedly when she learned who the caller was. She was thrilled at being interviewed by a big city newspaperman— especially one whose stories she had been reading with avid interest daily. Saxon's questions made her feel very important, and the reporter's easy-going, bantering tone sounded almost flirtatious. She leaned over backward to be helpful and told him all she knew about Vita's job and her friendships with John and Herbert.

When Saxon asked whether Vita had known or worked with Carol Forsythe, the murdered actress, Claire hesitated.

"You say Miss Reynolds worked with a number of actresses on the TV commercials, didn't you?" he asked persuasively.

"Yes."

"Well, Miss Forsythe did a lot of work at the same studio and she lived just a few blocks away. So it's quite possible they knew and worked together, isn't it?"

"Yes," Claire said easily persuaded. "Oh, I think it's quite possible."

They chatted a few minutes longer and Claire felt a little sorry when the conversation ended. The reporter had a charming voice and she had enjoyed it. After it was over, she found herself too stimulated to go back to sleep. Instead she went back over their conversation as she had breakfast, even though it was only four-thirty.

72

13

THE MOTORCYCLE COP patrolling the area near Vita's house looked carefully at everybody walking the streets. In Beverly Hills walking through a residential district at 4 A.M. would have seemed extremely suspicious. But in Hollywood, on the Sunset Strip, the bars had closed just a little earlier and it was not too unusual. All the same, he had had instructions from Lieutenant Goldberg to check everybody who did not look absolutely right to him. And especially all men walking alone.

He stopped a few men and asked them if they lived in the neighborhood. Nearly all did. One, embarrassed, said he didn't—that he had just left his girl friend. The officer smiled and nodded. The man looked relieved and offered him a cigarette which the policeman accepted. Neither noticed the man who rounded the corner a few yards away accelerating his pace when he saw them.

The man wandered into each dark alley between houses, looking for a lighted window. There was none. He turned into the next block and checked a whole row of one-story stucco dwellings. The fourth from the corner showed a lighted window. He crept into the alley and approached the window. The blind was nearly down to the bottom, but not quite. He could, by pressing his face to the window ledge, see clearly what was going on.

There was a pretty, dark girl of about seventeen or eighteen and a boy a couple of years older. They were on the living-room sofa, kissing. A minute later the boy tried to put his hand under the girl's dress. The watcher in the darkness outside pressed his face closer. The girl stopped the boy the first time he tried to put his hand under her dress. Not the second.

A moment later the boy whispered something in the girl's ear. She shook her head violently.

"Aw come on," the boy said out loud.

"No, Peter. You know I don't do it."

"Why not? Your old man's not due for another couple of hours. Don't you like me?"

"Sure I like you. If I didn't I wouldn't even kiss you."

"You've done it before, haven't you? You told me."

"Just once," the girl said. "I thought I loved the man."

"Oh, so it was a man. What's the matter—I'm not old enough?"

"Peter, you're being stupid about the whole thing. I just don't want to go to bed with you. That's all."

"You don't like me," the boy said. "I'm just some God-damn creep you see when you got nothing better to do. Okay. If that's how you want it." He got up angrily.

She pulled him down quickly and kissed him. "Honest to God, Peter, you're crazy. Would I have let you do what you did if I thought you were a creep? I like you. I like you better than anyone I know. I just don't want to make love—" She hesitated. "Not tonight anyway. Please don't insist. I know my father's not due yet, but I get nervous sometimes thinking what he'd do if he ever caught us. He's got a wild temper."

"Oh, Jesus," the boy said disgustedly. "How I hate these damned weasel-worded females. If you were a virgin I'd understand."

"Please, Peter." She was silent a moment. "Would you like it better if I took off my dress?"

The boy smiled. "Keep going."

"Just down to my brassiere and panties," she warned.

The watcher saw the girl rise and pull the dress over her head. Then she took off her slip. Now she was wearing a pair of navy blue panties and a brassiere. The watcher's eyes widened. The boy smiled at the girl and said, "Jesus, you're beautiful. Take off the brassiere too."

"Just the brassiere." She allowed him to remove it. When he had tossed it on the sofa, the boy crushed her in his arms. They sat down and he began to caress her slowly, lovingly, fondling her small, pear-shaped breasts and her long, well-shaped legs. The watcher sucked in his breath and stared hungrily at them.

The girl received his caresses placidly, letting her pliant body respond to his excited fingers. "Are you sure no one can see us?" she asked. "There's a nosy neighbor next door—she's always sticking her nose in the window."

"You go in often for this indoor sport?" the boy said, holding one of her breasts in his hand. He tried to pull off her panties. She stopped him. "The answer is no to both questions," she said laughing. "I told you only the brassiere."

"Just take them off. I won't try anything. I just want to see you."

74

"You've seen enough; don't be a hog," she said pleasantly.

The boy said nothing, but a few minutes later, he jerked at her panties again, pulling them down over her thighs. The watcher outside stared at them and dug the fingernails of his right hand into the palm of his left. His breath came faster as he watched the boy continue to try to pull the girl's panties off. She resisted and for a moment they wrestled on the sofa. The girl threw him off finally. The boy leaped on her again and kissing her, struggled with her underwear. Her panties fell to her ankles. The watcher outside felt a dizzy feeling in his head. He wanted to touch the girl's body so badly it was almost unbearable. He hated the boy and was dying to be in his place. To fondle the girl's beautiful breasts and legs himself.

"You've ripped my pants," the girl said angrily as she threw the boy off a second time. She raised the panties to her hips with as much dignity as she could muster. She looked beautiful to the watcher as she stood erect, her firm breasts jutting out stiffly from her slim torso.

"I think you'd better go, Peter," she said. "I told you I didn't want that before we started."

"Christ, I should have known I had a damned teaser on my hands," he said loudly and bitterly.

Outside the watcher continued to stare at the almost-naked girl, so raptly he had not moved for fifteen minutes. Suddenly he heard the putt-putt of a motorcycle and started to run into the back of the alley behind the house so the police flashlight could not find him. A moment later the motorcycle had passed and he crept back to his old position.

The sound of his footsteps had frightened the girl.

"You hear that?" she said anxiously.

"Yes," he said, a little frightened.

"It may be my father," she wailed. "You'd better get out of here."

She looked worriedly at him. "The back way. Quickly."

"But there isn't any more noise," he said. "What are you worried about?"

"He may be spying on us," she said. "He doesn't trust me and I think he does that sometimes. Are those blinds down really, all the way?"

"Yes," the boy lied.

"Please go. Call me tomorrow night." She kissed him hurriedly.

The boy ran into the kitchen and out the back door. Outside he dimly saw a figure standing by the window, a tall figure with what appeared to be a cigarette holder in its mouth. In a panic, the boy darted toward the rear and past the darkened hulk of the house and ran out of the alley of the next building into the street.

A moment later the watcher moved around to the back door, turned the handle softly and went inside. He closed the door behind him and moved quietly to the living room. The room was dark, but he could see a light in a room in a small hallway behind it. He pushed the door open and walked in. The girl was in a small bathroom next to the bedroom. The door was slightly ajar and he could hear a shower running.

"Papa, is that you?" she called. "I'll be right out. I wasn't able to sleep so I started reading. Then it got so hot I decided I needed a shower. I'll be right out." The shower stopped. "How come you're home so early tonight, Papa?" The girl waited a minute. "Papa?"

The watcher pushed the door of the bathroom inward and walked in. He saw the girl drying her body with a large Turkish towel. She was moving it briskly across her breasts when she saw him enter. Her eyes grew wide with fear as she saw him. In an instinctive gesture of modesty she wrapped the towel around her waist and breasts, but he could see the well-buffed redness of the glowing flesh beneath and above it.

Before she could speak, he ripped it from her body and threw it on the floor. She tried to run past him out the door, but he caught her, smiling, and began to cup her breasts with one hand, holding her close to him with the other. Suddenly the girl began to scream and he removed the hand from her breast and clamped it over her mouth.

"Don't scream," he said. "Don't scream. I won't hurt you. I just want to touch you. Like your boy friend." He held the naked girl close in the crook of his arm, the palm smothering the scream while his other hand cupped her small buttock. A minute later he put the hand around her throat and squeezed it a little.

"If you scream I'll have to do that," he warned. "Let's go on the bed. He carried the girl in his arms into the bedroom and lay her gently on the bed. A second later he was running his hands up and down her body. The girl shuddered as his fingernails dug into her thighs and in her terror and pain, she forgot his warning. She screamed out loud. The watcher's hands leaped to her throat immediately and the strong fingers slowly strangled the girl. Then he jumped from the bed and rushed out the back door.

In the next house, the girl's neighbor woke up when she heard the scream. But she was not sure what it was. She thought it might be a frightened cry in a nightmare. She listened closely and when no new sound came, she shrugged and went back to sleep.

As Lieutenant Goldberg stretched out in his bed, Herbert Buhler popped into his mind. Was there any possibility that he might be the prowler? He shook his head. "I'm crazy," he thought.

But the thought kept him awake. Was it really crazy? Sure Buhler was a schoolteacher. What difference did that make? Anybody could turn into a psychotic personality. Besides, what did they know about him? Goldberg groaned. It was like turning over a rock and watching slimy things crawl out. He would put a tail on Buhler in the morning, he decided. He slept like a baby until seven o'clock when Farley called him to tell him a girl had been raped and murdered six blocks from Vita's house.

Goldberg hung up, dressed quickly, not daring to look at the resentful face of his awakened wife, and went down to his car. The girl's house was a cheap stucco dwelling set in a row of identical single-story houses. Tiny alleys barely wide enough to permit cars to drive through to garages in the rear, separated the houses. When the detective arrived, two uniformed policemen were already there. He nodded briskly to them and went inside. He could hear a man sobbing as he entered the dark foyer into the crowded living room.

"Hello, Lieutenant," a man in civilian clothes said. "This is the girl's father. Mr. Pandowski. He found the body."

Goldberg took a long look at the sobbing middle-aged fat man on the chintz-covered sofa and felt a little sick.

"Come into the bedroom, Tommy," Goldberg said, "I want to see her and you can fill me in."

The two detectives entered the small bedroom, leaving the fat man alone with his grief. Goldberg looked at the bed. On it lay a slim teen-aged dark-haired girl, naked and dead. Her brown eyes stared at the ceiling and she seemed to be gasping for breath. Next to the body was a pair of navy blue panties, ripped at the top.

Goldberg examined the body professionally, noting the scratches on the girl's breasts and on her thighs.

"Rape?" he asked.

"The medical examiner says no."

"Tell me about it."

77

"The father came home from work about half an hour ago and found her. All he knows is she had a date to go to a party with some college boy she went around with. We're bringing him down. He swears he didn't do it."

Goldberg nodded. Mother of God, he was thinking, how long is this going to go on? If they didn't bring in a suspect soon, he'd be ashamed to show his face in the station house.

"I'm going to look around," he said. He examined the bedroom carefully, looking for something. He was not sure what. It was only in the movies or TV that criminals thoughtfully left you their calling cards, he thought bitterly. The other man went back into the living room.

Goldberg looked at the girl again, this time unprofessionally, sadly. The dead girl looked the age of his daughter, Francie, who was in her freshman year at San Jose College. She looked like most of the high-school seniors he saw trooping into the fancy ice-cream parlors in Hollywood or Beverly Hills, pretty girls with long legs and slim waists and small, promising breasts. The kind of girls, he thought sadly, who were made to order for two-seater sport cars, blue jeans, beach parties and long telephone conversations about their favorite boys and teachers.

He stopped wool-gathering and went to the telephone near the bed. He called the station house and spoke crisply to a detective.

"Goldberg here. Eddie, get a stake-out on Herbert Buhler. Lives in Hollywood. Name is in the book. B-u-h-l-e-r. See if he's home and find out where he was an hour ago if you can. I'll call you later."

The other detective came in as he hung up.

"The kid's here. You want to talk to him here or in the kitchen?"

"The kitchen," Goldberg said wearily. His eyelids felt as if they weighed a ton. I hope that idiot Francie knows how to take care of herself, he thought, as he went into the kitchen.

A twenty-year-old boy sat next to the green kitchen table. His thin, lanky frame was slightly crouched as if he expected a blow. His face was miserable. An iron-faced middle-aged uniformed officer was on the other side of the table. When Goldberg walked in, the boy looked frightened. The detective sat down on a scarred wooden chair near the stove and looked at him.

"No record on the boy, Lieutenant," the officer said. "He goes to UCLA—engineering. Admits he was with the girl but left before it happened."

Goldberg nodded. "Tell me everything you know," he said softly. "Don't leave anything out, please—even if it's embarrassing or you don't want her father to know. It'll come out anyway. And this is murder. Now take it from the time you got home with her."

The boy hesitated for a moment, swallowed hard and told his story.

"Were the blinds down?" Goldberg asked when the boy had told of his lovemaking.

"Yes, but there was about an inch or two open at the bottom because it was a hot night," the boy said.

The girl had made him leave quickly, he continued, and she had gone into her room. He sneaked out the back door carrying his shoes and looked around carefully. He had noticed a figure standing near the windows of the house.

"What did he look like?" Goldberg said.

"Well I couldn't see the face too well. It was dark, but he had something in his mouth. It looked like a cigarette holder. Long and thin. But it wasn't lit."

"Could you tell us how old he was, color of his hair or eyes," Goldberg asked.

The boy shook his head sorrowfully. It had been too dark.

"If you saw him again, could you identify him," Goldberg asked.

"I don't know. I think so," the boy said. He was trying to hide his terror at being involved in a murder case and anxious to prove how completely co-operative he wanted to be.

Goldberg nodded and stood up. "You can go home. We'll call you if we need any more information."

The boy's relief was so genuine, Goldberg could not help feeling sympathetic. As he turned to go into the living room, the girl's father rushed past him angrily and hit the boy with his fist.

"Son of a bitch, murdering bastard!" he screamed, sobbing, his tearstained face working compulsively. "You killed her. You raped her and killed her."

The detectives threw themselves between the grief-crazed father and the terrified boy. The officer led the boy to the back door of the house while the two detectives tried to calm down the older man.

"He didn't kill her," Goldberg said, as they led him back to the living room.

"Then who did?" the man asked. "Who? Who could do a thing like that? Who?" He began sobbing again. "How could anyone?"

Goldberg left the other detective to take care of the man and walked outside into the alley. The sun was beginning to feel strong already. The detective looked carefully at the windows that faced on the alley and looked at the ground beneath them. There were a couple of cigarette stubs, a card from a neighborhood television repair service and a piece of cellophane. He picked them all up.

"Nothing" he thought bitterly, "not a god-damned thing."

14

THE NEWS that Walter Johnson had been sneaking into his own house in the dead of night kept irritating Harvey Saxon during most of the night. But it was not till he learned of the new slaying in Vita's area, that he decided to check into the cameraman's habits. He called a studio publicist he knew from the Press Club and asked him what he knew about Johnson. The publicist was a little annoyed at being quizzed so early, but had learned to keep a honeyed voice when speaking to reporters. He told Saxon about Johnson's skill with glamor and sex.

Fifteen minutes later Saxon had learned that Johnson was in town and had been in three or four times during the last two weeks. He had left another number where he could be called. Johnson was flying back tonight, the publicist added.

Then Saxon called Goldberg and repeated what Mrs. McNulty had said about Johnson's sneaking in and out of his own house. He added a few words about Johnson's sexy photographic collection.

A few minutes later Farley and a uniformed policeman were on their way to an apartment house on Highland Avenue near the Hollywood Bowl.

They were admitted by a tall, shapely young blonde in a thin wrapper and fur-lined slippers. She acted frightened when she saw the police uniform.

"I'm Sergeant Farley," he said showing her his badge. "May I speak to Mr. Johnson, please."

"There's no one here by that name," she said unconvincingly.

"Can we come in?" Farley asked. She nodded and involuntarily glanced at a closed door in the rear of the apartment.

Farley moved quickly to the door and flung it open, standing to one side. The policeman stood on the other side, the woman stood a few feet away, staring at them.

"Don't shoot," she yelled. "He's not armed."

"When the door opened they saw a tall, thin man on the bed. He was dressed in a pair of pink shorts with blue robins dancing on them. He jumped off the bed, his face full of consternation as he saw Farley.

"What the hell is this?" he asked. Then he paled as a light dawned on him. "You bitch, you told me he was in San Francisco."

The man looked as if he expected Farley to hit him.

"That's not my husband," the blonde said. "They're both policemen. They came here to see you."

"Police? What for?" the astonished man said.

"If you're Walter Johnson, you'd better get dressed and come down to the station with me. We've got some questions we want to ask you."

Johnson still looked bewildered. "Is this some kind of gag? Look, mister. I don't know who cooked up this thing. But I haven't done anything."

The woman threw him a red robe she took from a hook behind the door. "Put this on, you damned fool. I told you not to stay here. They were probably sent down by Steve." He put on the robe quickly.

Johnson looked uncomfortable. "What the hell is this all about? A divorce raid or what? I never heard of police being called in before. This isn't a hotel. It's a private apartment." He was beginning to recover from his earlier shock.

"It's got nothing to do with the lady," Farley said. "I'm working on the prowler case. We want to check on your whereabouts for the last few days."

"My what?" Johnson looked astounded. "You think I killed those women?"

"I didn't say you did. The girl who lives below you was threatened last night and another girl was killed this morning not far away. You were seen sneaking into your house at one A.M. this morning and you've been up there several times without showing a light. Why?"

Johnson looked embarrassed and said nothing.

"I'll give you a few minutes to get some clothes on, Mr. Johnson," Farley said. His nerves were frayed and the latest strangling had made him very irritable.

"You arresting me?" Johnson said incredulously.

"We want to check your whereabouts on several dates

81

you've been in town. If you're clean you have nothing to worry about."

"But I'm supposed to start shooting a picture near Sacramento tomorrow morning and I've got to be there late this afternoon."

"Oh, Jesus. If this gets in the papers," the woman yelled.

"Shut up, Molly," Johnson said. "Look, officer, can we keep this thing quiet? I've been here every day I've been in town. I came down a few times when they stopped shooting because of casting or other problems."

"Where've you stayed when you were in town?" Farley asked. The man hesitated. "Here," he said reluctantly.

"Shut up," the woman screamed. "He's lying. He's never been here before. I never saw him before last night. I was drunk and he brought me home."

"Molly, don't say that," Johnson pleaded. "This is a murder investigation. I don't want my wife to know about this either. But for Christ sakes, I can't do anything about it."

"He's right," Farley said. "You're the best alibi he could have if it's true. You've been here all the time?"

"Yes," Johnson said. "I've known Molly for months and the last few visits I've stayed here with her. Reason I stole into my own house late was to get cash. Naturally I didn't want Vita to know I was in. She would have wondered why I didn't stay at home or talk to her."

"If you can make a sworn statement to that at the station, and it checks, you have nothing to worry about," Farley said, looking at the woman. She looked unhappy. "Isn't there any way I don't get mixed up in this. My husband'll kill me if he finds out. Not only that. It'll kill me for pictures. The only reason I did this was Walter arranged a screen test for me next week. If this gets out—"

Farley shrugged. "I can't guarantee anything."

Suddenly the woman's anger flared. "You son-of-a-bitch," she shouted at Johnson. "I'll go through with this to save your neck. But don't ever come near me again. I'll spit on you next time I see you. I'll be dressed in five minutes, officer!" She flounced off angrily into the bathroom and slammed the door.

Johnson shook his head as he put on his pants. "The Goddamn joke is I haven't done a thing. Not a damned thing. Just because I go into my own house for a few things, I'm a murderer. I have nothing to worry about, the man says." He shook his head. "Nothing except breaking up a marriage of twenty years standing."

Farley had sat beside the girl's bed all night after taking a Benzedrine pill. Vita slept quietly under the doctor's sedation. Farley was struck by the girl's simple loveliness. He felt as if he were looking at a beautiful sculptured head. Vita's dark, thick hair was sprawled across the white pillow and the planes of her face were in repose as she slumbered. Farley could not help admiring the cupid's bow made by her thin, red lips, or the pert, childish nose and the tiny ears whose delicate, pink color intrigued him.

When the precinct called to inform him of the new killing, the telephone's ring jarred her out of her sleep for a moment, but there was no sobbing. He talked to Goldberg a moment later, almost whispering the news.

When the doctor arrived at nine-thirty, he made a quick examination and shook his head.

"I think we'd better get her to the hospital. She's still in hysteria."

Vita began to tremble again and sob. The doctor gave her another injection. Then he ordered an ambulance.

When the doctor left with Vita in the ambulance, Farley went to the telephone and called his nephew at home. The boy answered sleepily.

"What's the matter, Tony?" Farley asked. "You sit up and watch all the late movies on TV?" Sometimes the boy watched them until after two A.M.

"No, Jim," he said. "I went to a movie and then I sort of wandered around. I went to a few bars up on Sunset Strip and around Laurel Canyon. I couldn't sleep."

"I'm sorry," Farley said, trying to ignore a small knot of fear in his stomach. "I meant to get home for dinner."

"Oh, that's okay, Jim, I know you're busy. We'll have fun after you get through with the case. Maybe we can go fishing in Ensenada."

"Yeah, sure," Farley said. "So you just kept wandering around, huh? How late were you up?"

"Oh, I don't know, Jim. I closed out one of the places, then I walked home. Don't worry about it, feller. I've done it before. I just can't sleep sometime and I feel like seeing warm bodies."

"Sure," Farley said. "Are you going to church now?"

"Yes, I thought I'd go there for a while," Tony said.

Farley hesitated. "Mind if I go with you?"

"Okay. Be good to see you."

Farley hung up and went out to the car. He was worried about his nephew's increasing depressions.

83

The detective and the boy entered the church quietly. Farley hesitated, not wanting to disturb the boy, yet feeling that he must speak to him.

"Did you see the psychiatrist yesterday?" he asked Tony.

The boy nodded sadly. "I saw him. Jim, why don't I just quit? After all, I'm a Korean War hero, even if they did boot me out as a psycho."

"Stop it. I don't want to hear you talk like that," Farley said.

"I just don't want to be a burden," the boy said.

"I don't mind the expense," Farley spoke softly. "What you been doing lately, Tony?"

"Oh, nothing much. I go to the library or take long walks."

"Where do you walk?" the detective asked sharply.

"I usually walk around Hollywood Boulevard in the daytime. At night I drive up to Laurel Canyon, park the car and walk there. I haven't been picked up for peeping at naked women, if that's what you mean."

"I didn't mean that. You were only picked up for loitering, and then the whole thing was dismissed."

"Then what the hell are you checking on me now for?" The boy's eyes widened in sudden comprehension. "Jesus! You brought me here to grill me about that prowler up in Laurel Canyon. Ever since I was picked up in that alley you've been worrying about me. You still think I went there to watch that woman undress."

"I do not. Sit down and stop acting foolishly. I was a little worried because you do get those strange daydreams and wander around so much. But that's all I was worried about."

Tony looked horrified. "My own uncle thinking I'm a dirty pervert." He got up quietly and walked toward the door. . . .

Goldberg was sitting at his desk eating a sandwich when Farley walked in. He offered half to Farley, who shook his head.

"Sit down, Jim," Goldberg said, scowling. "We got bad news. It looks as if our friend did this one too."

"Are you sure?"

"Positive. Same technique, same bruises and no penetration."

Farley looked stunned. "But how? We had patrols in the whole area. He'd be crazy to try it."

"He is crazy." Goldberg said. "Sure we had patrols. But you can't watch every inch of every block." He was angry with himself more than with anyone else. "There isn't any doubt that this guy's a psycho." He noticed Farley's lips tighten. "What's the matter, don't you agree?"

"Of course," Farley said. He decided not to repeat his conversation with his nephew.

"The way I see it, the prowler was scared off by the cops around Vita's block. He was all jazzed up sexually, or maybe he was drunk and he was all primed. So he wanders off about six or eight blocks and attacks another girl. How's Vita, by the way?"

"They took her to the hospital," Farley said. He felt guilty at hiding Tony's conversation from him.

Goldberg said, "Several murders in two weeks. One plain rape and another sent to the hospital in a hysterical condition. What a score. And that jerk who calls from City Hall to keep the mayor informed has been talking to the Commissioner all morning."

Farley nodded sympathetically. "The DA on your head too, chief?"

"Called twice already. The newspapers are on his tail and the Mayor's office. I'm the goat naturally since I'm handling the case."

"Do we have anything to go on at all, chief?"

"I don't know. I have an idea. But it's probably a crazy one."

"What is it?" Farley said.

"Buhler," Goldberg said softly.

"Buhler?" Farley looked doubtful. "But he's in love with the girl."

"You ought to study psychology instead of law." Goldberg said testily. "He's in love with her, but can't get her. He's a little nuts on the subject of sex. Thinks about it day and night."

"How do you know that?"

Goldberg told him about Buhler's dates with his pupils.

"That's hearsay, chief," Farley objected. "You can't go by that. Every time we get a case like this, we throw out a dozen leads like that."

"I know. I know. But it could be that Buhler's a schizo or whatever you call it."

Goldberg bit off the end of a cigar thoughtfully. "I'm having him tailed, Jim. He may be clean, but something about the guy keeps worrying me. Especially that story about his feeling up a fifteen-year-old girl in his class, and taking her home.

"Why don't you shoot up to the school and nose around. Talk to the principal and this McNulty girl and maybe you can interview the little Green girl. If this guy is taking high-school girls up to his place and playing with them the bastard shouldn't be teaching anyway. I'll be over at Stevens if you want me."

15

Two HOURS LATER, Lieutenant Goldberg was sitting opposite J. B. Dennison, the spectacled, white-shirted and neutral-faced executive director of the Stevens Dairy. The detective, wearing a crumpled blue suit and still looking a little tired from an active night, had just explained his visit.

"This prowler, if it is him, may call her here. He knows where she works and it's quite possible. I want to have a man monitor everything that comes in for her."

The stout executive looked doubtful. "Well, we all want to help, but I don't see how those girls in there are going to be able to do any work with a policeman in there all day."

Goldberg lit a cigar and puffed at it thoughtfully. "Look, Mr. Dennison. I know this is busting up your routine, but it's my duty to find this character—to clobber him before he commits another attack or murder."

Dennison looked thoughtful. "Well sure, and I want to help. I just want to keep the disturbance down to a minimum. There's been too much excitement already. Have you seen the afternoon papers?" He pushed them over to Goldberg.

The entire story was on the front page, with a banner headline. It told about John Palmer's arrest, Vita's habits of entertaining late and mentioned that Vita's mother was gravely ill in Sioux City where the news had reached her.

When Goldberg finished the story, he sighed and looked apologetically at Dennison.

"It's a good story. Harvey ought to write fiction. But there isn't much truth in it."

"You mean he just made it up?" Dennison said, getting a little angry. "If he did he can be sued for libel. Just for the things he's said about my employees and giving the company that kind of publicity."

The detective shook his head. "He didn't exactly make it up. There is some truth in it. But Harvey's trying to make a big story out of it. He's an ambitious boy from Chicago.

The business about the lovers' quarrel—it's strictly from Sam Goldwyn. But there is an element—mind you I say just an element—of truth there. Her parties—that's a lot of malarky. It's the sort of thing you get from nice middle-aged women who get talked to by reporters for the first time in their lives. They saw her light on a few times after ten or heard some music. Maybe some guy was seen kissing her good night, so to them she's throwing wild parties. The business about how the caller may have been an irate suitor. That's for the birds. I can just see Harvey reaching out like mad to build up the story. About her mother, I don't know."

Dennison shook his head. "No matter how much truth there is in it," he said, "it's terrible. We've never had anything like this happen in this company. And it couldn't have happened at a worse time. We're expecting our board of directors here from New York tomorrow."

"I'm sorry," Lieutenant Goldberg said.

"How's Miss Reynolds?" Dennison asked as Goldberg rose.

"She's still pretty bad," Goldberg said. "They have a nurse with her all the time. That kind of thing really gets them."

"You mean she's—she's mentally, well, deranged?" Dennison asked, surprised. "You mean she's liable to do something, like suicide?"

"I don't know," the detective said honestly. "I'm not a doctor. But hysteria—that can lead to anything. They don't know what they're doing. They have to be watched or you're liable to find them trying to climb out the window. Well I'd better run along. Got work to do. I'll have to talk to the girls in Miss Reynolds' office."

He got up, took his hat from the desk and ambled slowly out the room. Behind him Dennison looked very worried.

As he approached Helen Wright's office, Goldberg heard Farley call him. The Irishman looked tired but there was a brightness in his eyes.

"You talk to the girls yet?" he asked.

"No, let's go. You get anything?"

"I haven't been able to get to the little Green kid, but I got an earful from her friend Joan. Carlotta called her yesterday and told her Buhler had picked her up after school and taken her home. He made her take off her clothes, played with her for a couple of hours and palmed her off with twenty bucks."

"Holy mackerel!" Goldberg said. "Did you talk to Carlotta?"

"I can't get hold of her. She told Joan she was going up

to Santa Barbara for the day with her mother and the latest boy friend. He's got a boat up there. She'll be back tomorrow."

"Doesn't she have to be in school?" Goldberg asked.

"Sure. But from what I've learned about Carlotta, that never stopped her from doing anything. I picked up quite a bit about Herbert too, but that can wait. Let's go on in."

John Palmer had been in his office just a few minutes when Goldberg called from Helen's office to say he was coming up. The advertising manager felt very tired and wished he had time to go around the corner for a drink. He had thought often of caching a bottle in his drawer or having a small office bar for himself and visiting firemen, as he used to in New York. But the Stevens Dairy was such a damned museum that they almost crabbed if you smoked in the office.

He had had a trying night and morning. First the disgusting experience of being tossed into the tank like a common drunk and spending the night lying on a bunk near the ceiling with a crowd of drunks and drifters who had been picked up for various petty offenses. He had wanted to stay until he appeared before the judge, since it was only a simple assault charge. The last thing he wanted to do was ask Ginny for help. But when morning came and he was still there, he became edgy. He had to discuss the new magazine and television contracts with Dennison that afternoon and he would have to get home and change first. As the morning passed, he became more and more irritable. But no one knew when he would be released. A trusty said he might even be there till nightfall.

Finally he telephoned Ginny, embarrassed, feeling foolish and uncomfortable. She was furious at the bad publicity and the plea for help nearly stuck in his craw. He could hear her chortling with amusement and getting ready to crow over his red-faced discomfort. He called Vita's home and was miserable when he learned that the girl was in the hospital in a hysterical state. Then he was crestfallen when a trusty showed him a newspaper with Saxon's story about the fracas in Vita's house. He was dumbfounded because somehow he had never really believed that a Los Angeles newspaper could front-page such a story. He had been sure that if it were used at all it would be buried in a paragraph in the back pages.

He was taking some aspirin when Goldberg walked in. The detective smiled sympathetically. "You look the way I feel," he said.

John shook his head. "I wouldn't want to trade places. I just heard about that other murder. You must have a nice job."

"Yeah," Goldberg said. "I'd rather milk rattlesnakes. I'm sorry I had to toss you into the tank, but you insisted on being a middleweight. Did you ever do any boxing? That was a nice left hook you used on Buhler."·

"Some in college," John said sheepishly.

"Can you tell me anything about Vita or anybody she knows that might help?" Goldberg said coming to the point. "I mean, you do know her pretty well." He held up his hand as he saw John bridle. "I didn't mean it that way, simmer down." John shook his head. "Okay. I just thought I'd ask." The secretary walked in to announce that there was a call in her office for the detective.

In the secretary's office, Goldberg was talking to Farley, who was calling from Vita's house. The policewoman who had been detailed to answer Vita's telephone had received a call.

"Mary thinks it might have been the prowler," Farley said. "He sounded very confused."

"What did he say?" Goldberg asked.

"Oh just general stuff like where was she. He hadn't read the papers apparently. Said he was just a friend—but wouldn't give his name."

"Did he try to get, you know, familiar with Mary?"

"No. He only·talked for a minute or two and Mary kept stalling him. I traced it to a bar about a mile from here. There was also a call from a newspaper in Iowa."

That did it, Goldberg thought. Vita had been afraid of her mother knowing more than anything. Now the hometown paper was on the story. They were probably calling her mother right now. It was like tossing a pebble into a pond, he thought. The ripples get wider and wider. Everybody involved in a case like this feels the shock, he thought sadly, even when they were thousands of miles away. A sex crime hurts the victim's friends and family almost as much as it does her.

16

HARVEY SAXON called Claire about three o'clock. He had been given a strong pat on the back by the managing editor for his story and told to get a follow-up. Since the editor had liked the details about Vita's interest in Palmer and his fight with Buhler, he decided there was more pay dirt in that area. His brief conversation with Claire, her nervous excitement at being interviewed, gave him an idea. He would have to protect his contact with her to get anything the other papers couldn't.

"I want to thank you very much for your kindness last night," he told her, his voice full of gratitude and warmth. "I felt badly about calling you at that hour and several times I wanted to hang up and let you go to bed, but—" his voice hesitated and then lowered to a whisper. "There was a quality, a warmth about your voice that kept me on the hook. It's pretty lonely working on the graveyard shift. You generally hear nothing but drunks and dull types who want information. When you hear a rich, warm voice that promises so much, well, you kind of want to hear more . . ." His voice trailed away embarrassedly. "I'm sorry. I forgot you were in your office."

Claire, who dated men only about half a dozen times a year, was fascinated.

When Saxon asked her if he might come by before work that evening because he was terribly lonely and knew no one else in town, she only hesitated a minute. His weak excuse— that he wanted her to read a draft of his follow-up story was enough to overcome a certain fear of his aggressiveness. She spent most of the remainder of the workday feeling fluttery inside and a little weak in the knees.

At five-thirty that evening, a smiling Harvey Saxon walked into Goldberg's office. The detective, who was alone, regarded him sourly.

"Who are you knifing next, Harvey?" he asked.

"What's that junk you're playing with, Lieutenant?" Harvey asked pleasantly. There were cigarette stubs and cellophane on Goldberg's desk. "Clues to the killer?"

The detective shrugged and slipped them into his desk drawer.

"All right, who's your latest victim?" he asked wearily. "You wouldn't be up here grinning like a Cheshire cat if you hadn't got a line on somebody."

"Could be," Saxon said, grinning. "Can I talk to you alone?"

"Sure. Nobody ever comes in here except reporters with hot pants."

"Where's Farley?" Saxon asked.

"He's out checking something. Why?"

"This concerns him, that's why." Saxon said softly.

Goldberg looked up sharply. "What are you trying to say?"

Saxon sat on a corner of the desk. "I've been doing a little digging into the files on all the sex offenders pulled in in the last few months. I discovered that his nephew was picked up for peeping up in the Hollywood area. The case was quashed but . . ."

"How'd you find out then?" Goldberg asked quietly, not taking his eyes away from the newsman.

Saxon shrugged. "Look, in my business you make a lot of friends. I know the thing was quashed. But I heard about it anyway. I just thought you'd like to know."

Goldberg stood up slowly and grabbed the reporter's lapel.

"Listen, Harvey. I can't stop you from using that. But if that ever sees print, I'll kill you with both hands. So help me God." He tightened his grip on Saxon's coat.

"That kid never did a wrong thing in his life. He was loused up by a stupid, nervous bag who lied. The boy's a Korean veteran and he was shaken up pretty badly by being in a Chinese prison. You print that and you'll kill him. To say nothing of what it will do to Farley."

Saxon stared at the detective's flushed, angry face and tore his coat away.

"Look, don't threaten me, Lieutenant. I don't like it."

"You going to use that about Farley's nephew?" Goldberg asked quietly.

"I don't know yet," Saxon said. "Maybe I will and maybe I won't. It's a good yarn. How one of the top detectives on the case must feel having a nephew who was picked up for a sex offense in the same area." He moved back as Goldberg edged toward him. "Un-uh, Lieutenant. No mayhem. It might make an even better story to have a member of the press attacked by an angry detective."

"Get out of here, you bastard," Goldberg said. "Don't ever come near me. If you want to complain to the captain, go ahead. And if they want my job they can shove it up their ass."

Saxon tried to smile. "It might help me forget Tony altogether if you gave some more leads on the other people involved. I'm trying to knock out a new background feature on this case every day. Christ, you know what this series means to me. I need material."

"You mean give you some dirt about some other poor slob so you can lay off poor Farley's nephew?" Goldberg said acidly.

He shook his head. "How does it feel being a whore, Saxon? Or should I say a vulture? That's really what it is, isn't it—picking at the bodies?"

The reporter flushed, stung by Goldberg's words.

"It's what people want to read, Goldberg. I don't create people's tastes," he said defensively. He turned suddenly as the door opened to admit Farley.

"Hi, Saxon," the Irish detective said genially. "Still digging?"

Saxon blushed and shook his head as he walked out.

"What's the matter with him?" Farley asked.

Goldberg said nothing.

At seven o'clock Harvey Saxon entered Claire Bronson's flat and a moment later was making them both double Scotches on the rocks. Claire hesitated. She drank only occasionally, and two drinks made her a little dizzy. But she decided that she could sleep it off when he left—probably an hour later. She was pleasantly surprised to note that the reporter was tall and good-looking, though he did seem a little too young for her. His brightness and electric smile warmed her but made her nervous.

Saxon had to hide his disappointment as soon as he saw her. She was too thin and too tall and her sallow, mousy face put him off. The only things about her that looked promising were the long legs and the breasts. The apartment was impossibly drab.

Claire seemed reluctant to speak about the case until after the third double Scotch. Surprisingly he had had no trouble offering her the third, only the second had bothered her. He was not worried about himself. He would take a tablet later which would keep him sober enough.

After the third drink, he was sitting with his arm around her on the sofa and Claire told him a little bit about Herbert Buhler, but she was slow on Palmer. Instead she began to feel sorry for herself and began talking about her abortive marriage which had failed ten years earlier. She had been married to a Texas businessman much older than she and he had stopped living with her soon after their wedding. The memory of how the man had simply stalked out of the house and taken to living with another woman still rankled. Harvey patted her head and caressed her arm understandingly.

He always got bored with weepy drunks. It was after nine and she had still not let anything drop that he could use. Maybe she would be more talkative in bed, he decided. And the Scotch was beginning to stimulate him too. He let his hand wander casually to her thigh. It was always easier to start there, he thought. With a woman like Claire, a sudden cupping of her breast might frighten her off.

"I hope you don't mind my talking about my marriage," Claire said, hardly aware of the hand on her lap, "I haven't mentioned it to anyone for years."

"Don't be silly," Harvey said softly and tenderly. "I'm interested in anything about you, Claire. I was interested the minute I heard your voice."

Claire smiled. It was the first time any man had even noticed she had a voice. The Scotch felt warm and she felt good with the reporter's arm around her waist. She giggled as his fingers moved along her leg.

"That tickles," she said, letting her head nudge his shoulder.

He kissed her suddenly, a warm, languid kiss, moving his tongue deftly between her teeth. Claire's face flushed a deep red as she put both arms around him. She felt weak in the knees. She made an ineffectual attempt to stop him when his hand cupped her breasts—the wire cups of her brassiere made Saxon's spirits droop a moment. I suppose they all wear them nowadays so they can all look like Jayne Mansfield, he thought gloomily.

He poured them another two drinks in the kitchen, watering his own carefully because he knew his limits. She sipped it greedily, enjoying the dizzy feeling in her head. She kissed Saxon warmly on the mouth.

"That's all for me. I don't want to get drunk," she said happily, blurring her words a little. His hand caressed the warm flesh of her thighs underneath the skirt, exciting her so much she put the almost-finished drink down. "No, please," she pleaded, "don't do that, Harvey," calling him by his first name for the first time. "Don't. That just drives me crazy. I'm not used to it any more."

"Let's go inside, darling," he whispered tenderly.

Claire reacted a little frightenedly. "No, please," she begged.

"I thought you liked me," he said in a sad, disappointed voice he had perfected years ago in Chicago.

"Oh I do, I do," she protested quickly, hugging him and ignoring the fact that her skirt was now high above her knees. "You don't want to make love to an old woman like me. I'm over forty. Nearly forty-five."

93

"That's the age a woman is at her loveliest, most charming," Saxon said, unbuttoning the top of her dress and kissing the cleavage of her breasts above the brassiere.

She buttoned herself quickly. "No, please. Not now. You have to go to work soon," she said almost frantically.

Saxon sighed. He played his trump card. He removed his shoes, trousers, shirt and shorts and sat beside her in nothing but an undershirt.

She stared at him through a haze as he embraced her, and did nothing to prevent him from unzipping her skirt and removing it. He bent to kiss her knees, hiding his disappointment at their boniness and the wiry black down on her thighs.

"Come on, baby, I won't hurt you," he said.

"Do you love me?" she asked in a begging tone, her eyes beseeching him.

"Of course," he said tenderly. "How could you even ask?"

"Please say it," she begged as he unbuttoned the top of her blouse again.

"I love you," he sighed.

She began to cry. "Oh, Harvey, you're wonderful. I haven't met anyone like you for ten years. Do you know what it's like to wait ten long years without anyone to love? The lonely nights I've spent alone, envying my married friends or even somebody like Vita having an affair with a married man."

Saxons ears pricked up at mention of Palmer and Vita. "What about him and Vita?" he said, holding her in his arms.

"Oh nothing," she said. "I don't know anything about them, but sometimes I lie in bed and imagine what their lovemaking must be like. How he holds her and warms her with his love and his arms." She tightened her arms around Saxon. "I've needed someone like you for so long. So long," she said, sobbing.

"Oh, Jesus," Harvey said to himself. Her weeping and slobbering were beginning to put him off. "Can you tell me anymore about Vita and Palmer? Have you heard anything that might indicate either Palmer or Buhler or any of her other boy friends might have made those calls to her? Are any of these guys neurotics or undergoing treatment?" His trained news mind was at work, trying to sift out anything of value that she might tell him.

"I don't know anything about her friends," she said weepily.

Saxon's heart sank. He had wasted his time. The brown, unhealthy pallor of her thin thighs did nothing to stimulate his desire. He shrugged and decided she was much more interesting above the waist.

"Let me take the blouse off and the other things," he said softly.

"No," she begged. "You won't like me. I don't have an interesting figure."

"It looks interesting to me. Especially here," he smiled, cupping her breast from the outside.

"No," she said looking at him, "you'll be disappointed." She hesitated, "unless you really love me. Do you?"

"Yes, dear, I do. Very much."

She rose, checked the blinds carefully to see they were completely down and took off her slip, her panty-girdle and was soon naked from the waist down. Harvey was a little surprised. Usually girls preferred to start from the top. She hesitated another moment, then sadly removed her blouse and the brassiere. She stood before him completely naked.

He could not contain his astonishment as he stared at her. Her breasts were nothing but tiny brown tips pressed flat against her chest. She was flatter than even a man, he thought. His desire vanished instantly as he looked at her.

Claire caught the look on his face and began crying. "I told you, I told you. My husband looked like that on my wedding night."

He looked embarrassed. But even if he had wanted to out of kindness, he could not make love to her. He turned away and put on his clothes, silently.

"You're leaving?" she said, taking his arm. "Oh, darling, I'm sorry."

"It's very late and I'm overdue at the office," he lied. All he wanted to do was get out of there fast and get to a bar where he could have a drink alone.

"Please don't go just like that," she begged. "Don't just walk out."

"I've got to go," he said looking at the floor. He went out the door.

She watched him go and then began sobbing violently, sitting on the sofa, naked and alone. Fifteen minutes later when the phone rang, she was still crying.

"What's the matter," she heard Helen Wright say. "Are you crying?"

"No," Claire said, "I just don't feel well."

"You sound very strange. Listen I called to tell you to be sure not to say anything to reporters. Mr. Dennison called me. They bothered him at his house and he's madder than a wet hen. He almost seemed to think it was Vita's fault. And maybe he's right if those stories are true. Did anyone call you?"

"No," Claire said, "nobody called me."

"You sound as if you had been drinking," Helen said. "Goodness, what is happening to everybody? I'll be glad when this mess is over. You go to bed. Do you want me to come over? Is it the back pain again?"

"No," said Claire, weeping, "it's not the back pain."

The city editor beckoned to Harvey Saxon as soon as he stepped into the editorial room. He slapped him on the back, beaming.

"You made it, Harvey," he said. "The old man okayed a raise this afternoon. And twice as much as you asked for. The guy was delighted. The features on the people tied in with the prowler scare really hit him. He's selling them to one of the big syndicates. You'll be in papers all over the country, and of course you'll get part of the take."

Harvey nodded slowly. He said nothing.

"What the hell's the matter with you, boy? Didn't you hear me. Your by-line's going to be spread across the damned country. I wouldn't be surprised if you don't get a bite from some magazine or publishing house to do a book on the case. The old man says he hasn't read such colorful background stuff since Damon Runyon. Aren't you pleased, for God's sake?"

Harvey nodded again and started to take off his coat before sitting down. His wooden expression did not change.

"Jesus, if that's the way you express pleasure, I'd hate to see you really get enthusiastic." He paused and then realized something. "I know what's bothering you. You're off the night shift as of tomorrow. Skipper's orders. He wants you to work full time on the prowler case and after that you do an exposé on rackets in California. With by-lines, naturally. Christ you may wind up a Pulitzer Prize winner yet." He looked at his watch. "What the hell are you doing here so early? You've got nearly an hour yet. Come on over to Tony's place and I'll buy you a drink. To celebrate."

At the bar, the city editor and one of his assistants kept up a patter of excited talk about the circulation boost caused by Saxon's pieces, and the assistant added that *Life* might pick the series up.

"They'd have to edit them a little, natch," he said, grinning. "Some of that stuff just skirted the ragged edge of the libel

96

law. Especially the piece on Johnson. I hear the studio suspended the poor bastard."

Harvey said nothing. The drink tasted bitter in his mouth and he left it alone after one sip. He wished the assistant city editor would shut up.

17

WHEN VITA left the hospital early the next morning, Farley tried to get her away from a battery of newsmen and photographers by hustling her to his car. He could not stop them from getting several pictures of a bewildered girl holding tightly to his arm.

"Do you plan to stay on in that house alone after the prowler's last threat," one reporter shouted as she brushed past him, "or are you going to move?"

"All right, boys, leave her alone," Farley said. "You can see she's still shaky."

"Do you think you may leave town?" another newsman yelled as she got into the car.

Vita sat back in the dark interior, trembling. "What does he mean, last threat? And why should I leave town?"

"Don't pay them any mind, Miss Reynolds," the detective said as they moved away from the curb. "They just want a story. You see the prowler or someone pretending to be him called you at the office several times and he said he hoped you hadn't left town because you were scared. The newspapers played it up big yesterday especially after—" His voice trailed away. He had started to tell her about the latest killing, but a look at the girl's expression stopped him.

"He called the office," she repeated blankly. "When?"

"Yesterday," the detective said. "He probably didn't know you were in the hospital until he read the newspaper story."

"It's been in the newspapers?" she said worriedly.

"And on radio and TV," Farley said apologetically. "You can't blame them. This is one of the worst prowler scares they've had in years. They know you had a close shave. And then there's that new threat."

"Do you think the story has been carried in the out-of-town newspapers?" she asked anxiously. "I wouldn't want my mother to hear about it."

"Oh there was something I wanted to tell you. Your uncle Fred wants you to call him when you get home."

"Uncle Fred?" she repeated. "Then they must have heard about it already. Poor Mother. I hope she hasn't had a relapse. Please, let's hurry, Mr. Farley."

The detective drove rapidly through the busy sun-filled streets. When they neared her block, he slowed down.

"You know it wouldn't be such a bad idea if you did go home for a while. Maybe a week or two," Farley said casually as he parked the car.

"Go home?" she said dully.

"I'm not trying to scare you, Vita," Farley said quietly. "But you've got to face the facts. There is a dangerous killer at large. He's tried to get to you once and he may again. We can give you a certain amount of police protection, naturally. But—"

"But you couldn't guarantee he wouldn't get through in some way."

"We'd have to give you a bodyguard around the clock," Farley said as he followed her into the house. "We can do that. I just thought you'd feel better being at home with your family until this thing dies down."

"I don't know," Vita said as she sat down on the living room couch. The familiar furniture in the room, the pictures on the wall and her unfinished novel, lying face down on the coffee table, seemed to deny everything that happened.

"Excuse me," Farley said. "Harry," he called out. A small, stocky man in his fifties with cropped gray hair and a stump of a cigar in his mouth came from the kitchen.

"This is Harry Plovers," he said as introduction. "He's monitoring your phone here. There's another man in your office. Harry will be relieved at night by another man. Your bodyguard should be due any minute."

As if on cue, the doorbell rang a moment later and a tall, husky red-faced man in civilian clothes came in. He had an Irish-looking face and a vacant, stupid grin on his face.

"This is Joe Blowston, Vita," Farley said. "He'll be with you all the time, except when he's relieved. He's able to take care of any emergency, so don't worry. Oh, by the way, does that couch open up as a bed?"

"No, why?" Vita asked surprised.

"Well Harry'll have to sleep somewhere. He wouldn't be any good if he had to sit up all night. But don't worry. He's a light sleeper."

"You mean he's going to stay here?" she asked, surprised.

Farley looked at Harry and Joe and laughed. "Look, Vita. Joe's going to be your shadow for the next few days. Where you go, he goes. If you go to the office, he'll go with you. If you stay home, he'll stay here. Of course Harry just stays here, if he wants a little rest, he can always lie down on the couch during the day."

"I hope you don't mind cigars, lady," Harry said in a hoarse voice. "I usually smoke on the job."

"Well is all this strictly necessary?" Vita said doubtfully. "I mean does he have to be with me all the time?" The reality of the situation was beginning to hit her unpleasantly. She was going to have to live with two or maybe four policemen twenty-four hours a day, seeing them all the time, having them with her everywhere.

"Look," Farley said, "we're dealing with a man who may be a maniac. He's already killed several women. I don't want you to be next. Joe doesn't actually have to hold your hand all the time. If you want to see someone alone just tell him. He'll back off, just staying close enough to be handy. Believe me, Vita. It's for your own protection. Please cooperate." Farley waited till the two men had gone into the kitchen. "There's another thing I'd like to ask you not to do. I'd rather you avoided seeing your Mr. Buhler for the next few days. Or if you see him, make sure Joe is with you."

Her eyes widened with astonishment. "Herbert Buhler?"

"It's just a hunch that Goldberg has. We both have. I may be wrong. But many people have been killed already. Just please stay clear of him until we give him a clean bill of health. Will you promise me that, Vita?"

"I can't do that unless you give me a better reason than that. I've known the man all my life. He's an old friend of my family." Vita was astounded that Farley could even think of Herbert as dangerous.

"All right," Farley said sighing. "I'm going to do something I don't like to do—tell you what I think before I've nailed it down. Your boy is apparently a little more off-balance than you think. He's done and said things that lead us to think he's a little unbalanced sexually."

"Herbert Buhler?" she said incredulously. "You don't know him. Why the slightest thought of sex would drive him into a corner. He's the most prudish, chaste man I've ever known and I've known him ever since I was a child. Heaven knows where you got that idea. I don't believe for a second that he could be capable of any sexual offense. It's crazy. I can't imagine why Lieutenant Goldberg should pick on him."

99

"There are other clues," Farley said gently. "We checked his apartment and found a huge stack of sexy magazines on the floor of a closet. Art studies, *Confidential* magazine, pinups. Stuff you'd expect to find in a bachelor's flat maybe. But when it's coupled with hell and brimstone lectures on evil to his classes—well it's a little funny."

"But Herbert Buhler is mortally afraid of sex. He dies if anyone so much as tells a smutty story. He shies away from it."

"That's how we see the prowler too," Farley said pointedly.

For the first time Vita realized the detective was speaking in deadly seriousness. "You really *do* suspect him of being the prowler," she said.

Farley shrugged. "He could be. It's all a question of degree. We know that whoever commits these crimes is sexually unbalanced. We know that he's able to get to these areas in the late afternoons. We know that he's not in any way conspicuous—doesn't excite any special attention. Buhler fits all these things." It might also fit his own nephew, he thought irritably.

"If you or Goldberg feel so strongly about Buhler, why haven't you arrested him?" Vita asked.

"Two reasons. We're still not positive and we don't like to make false arrests. He's being watched carefully while we do more checking. I'm sure about the fact that he's sexually unbalanced. I opened his desk yesterday while he was away and found several erotic books there. Nothing illegal, but it coincided with other things we learned. The reason I'm telling you all this is simply that I do not want you to take any chances."

In the excitement of hearing about Herbert, Vita had forgotten about Uncle Fred. She put the call through immediately. A few minutes later the operator called to say he had left and would return in three hours. She started to call her mother, but an intuitive feeling that she had better talk to her uncle first stopped her.

"Well, I've got to go," Farley said suddenly. He looked at the girl, pondering whether to say more. He shrugged and turned to her.

"There's something more you should know. I feel bad having to give you all this in one dose right after you've left the hospital. But you'd find out soon anyway. A young girl was murdered just six blocks from here, the night we were here waiting for him to show up. There's no doubt it was the prowler. Now you can see why I'm so worried about your taking care, why I would even advise you to go home for a while if you want to."

She nodded but said nothing.

"And there's another thing. "I've checked on Buhler's movements. He did not get home after he left here until three hours later."

Vita felt faint suddenly. Farley looked at her pale face and got her a glass of water. "Look, Vita. All I've told you is merely for your own protection. Actually nothing may happen. You're under constant guard and we're watching Buhler all the time. I just don't want you to take unnecessary chances. It may not be him at all. And the real one may be over the state line or the border by this time."

Vita nodded listlessly. "I think you ought to get some sun," Farley said. "I'll fix a chair for you out in front."

The detective looked a little remorseful as he led her outside. After he had left, Vita lay back in the sun and tried to relax. She listened to a swarm of bees playing tag with a rosebush and watched the street traffic. After an hour, she noticed the tall, lanky figure of the postman. Mr. Carter stopped to chat with her for a minute and said he was glad she was not hurt. A few minutes later, the footsteps of Mr. Alger, the "newsboy," awakened her. She looked up and saw his shy, friendly smile. As usual he was sucking on a lollipop. The sight of the lollipop in a grown man's face had always amused her. The young man came into the garden with the papers stacked neatly in the canvas pouch around his neck. He was a tall, thin man with dark, sparse hair and watery blue eyes. He passed by once a day to distribute free copies of a "throwaway" newspaper which featured rehashed day-old news stories on the front page and little more than neighborhood advertisements inside.

Vita said a few words to him nearly every day and knew him as well as the friendly Japanese gardeners who groomed the lawns and gardens of the houses on the block.

"Hello, Mr. Alger," she said. She liked to know everybody's name. The passion for anonymity in big cities always made her feel lonely.

"Afternoon, Miss Reynolds," the young man answered gently. "Good to see you home again. How're you feeling?"

"Tired," she said pleasantly, "but I'll be all right."

He removed a paper from the pouch and gave it to her. "Your story's right on page one. Sounds exciting."

101

"Thank you," she said. She read the story quickly. When she finished she felt as if her stomach would turn. It was all so awful. Especially the lies about John and Herbert. She looked up and noticed that Mr. Alger was watching her solicitously.

"Well I've got to finish these," he said softly and moved toward the garden fence. He turned at the gate. "You take care of yourself, hear? Don't go sitting too long in that sun. You're too nice a girl to get sick."

She smiled and nodded gratefully. Mr. Alger always seemed worried about her health and he looked as if he needed a good meal himself. He always seemed so lonely and eager to talk but he was too shy to linger more than a moment. Her mind switched back to the story in the paper. She wondered worriedly if her mother knew about the incidents. She rose quickly and entered the house. Farley was still talking on the phone. "They may have found him, Vita," he said slowly, when he finally turned to her.

"That was Lieutenant Goldberg. They picked up a man prowling around a house ten blocks from here and watching some woman undress. She saw him and started to phone the police but he went after her. Fortunately she screamed and her neighbors stopped him before he could do anything. Goldberg wants me to pick up the boy friend of the girl who was killed yesterday and bring him down. He may be able to identify the man."

He looked at the girl and hesitated. "Will you be all right?"

"Yes, I think so," Vita said tonelessly. "I think I'll just lie down and rest. I'm very tired. Please don't worry about me."

"I'll call you later," Farley said. She could feel his excitement. It was the same impatience that a hunter has when he's coming in for the kill. "I hope he's the man you want," she said.

"It looks like it could be," Farley said. "See you later."

After Farley left she dialed the number of her office and asked for John Palmer. He was out. She asked to speak to Helen Wright. Helen was politely interested in her health, but there was no mistaking her lack of warmth.

"Do you want me to come in today?" Vita asked. The thought of staying in the empty house was not appealing.

Helen hesitated and then said, "There's no hurry. Why don't you rest for a few days. Till you feel better. If you like, I can even arrange for you to get two or three weeks off, so you can go home and rest."

"I'm feeling fine now," Vita said. "I can be there this afternoon. The stuff on my desk is piling up. I had thought of coming in tomorrow, but I can just as easily start today."

"No, Vita, there's no need to hurry. I've given all your rush things to Claire." Helen's voice sounded a little nervous, embarrassed. "I think you'll be able to function better after you've had a good rest."

What's happened to me, she thought unhappily as she hung up the phone. Her entire life seemed to have been rocked by the prowler. He had affected her relationship with John, with Herbert, with the girls at the office and for all she knew had reached all the way to Sioux City. She had become involved with the police for the first time in her life and had become a central figure in the hunt for a notorious sex criminal. The notoriety had rubbed off on her and had made her persona non grata in her own office—a traffic hazard likely to hold up work.

She was interrupted suddenly by the telephone. She found herself trembling as she heard it ring. I'll never be able to hear another telephone ring without being scared to death, she thought. I'm even scared to pick it up now. She let it ring six times before she picked it up. It was John Palmer.

"How are you, baby?" he said. "Are you feeling all right."

"Yes," she said. It was good to hear his voice again. She realized how much she had missed him. "I'm sorry about what happened, darling. It must have been horrible for you. Being taken away like that."

"No. Forget about that, dear. I'm just worried about you. When I heard you were in the hospital I nearly went crazy."

"I'm all right, John. I guess I just need some rest. Are you going to come by?"

He groaned. "I wish I could, darling. I want to see you more than anything in the world. But Dennison had me on the carpet over that story in the papers and I think Ginny's hired a private detective to shadow me. You're the last person I want him to see me with. For your own sake as well as mine."

He told her that Dennison had warned him about the company's disapproval. John listened while she told him about the bodyguard and the newspapermen. "Oh my aching back," he said when she had finished. "It's better for both our sakes if we stop everything for a while. If I tried to cross Dennison or Ginny now, it would just mean trouble. And you're completely surrounded. It's hopeless."

103

Vita's heart sank. She had not bargained for anything like this.

"You mean you're not going to be able to see me at all or go ahead with the divorce?" She felt suddenly as if she were in prison.

John's voice sounded unhappy. "I think we can work out some way of seeing each other after this thing dies down—probably in a couple of weeks. But I think I'd better put away the divorce for a year. Otherwise Ginny'll insist on a messy court case. But at least we'll be able to see each other if we do it discreetly, darling."

"Don't bother," Vita retorted angrily. "If all you're worried about is your job, I'd rather not see you at all." She felt numb."

"It's only for a little while till all this notoriety dies down, Vita. What kind of dates do you think we could have with detectives or newsmen on our tail? It would be like holding hands in Union Station. Please try to see it my way, darling. I love you. But there's nothing we can do now." He paused, then added, "Darling, why don't you go home for a while. I know they'd okay it at the office. You'd be able to rest and by the time you're back, they may have solved the case. It'll all be over."

"Why does everybody want me to go home!" she said heatedly. "I don't need any rest. I'm not an invalid or a mental case."

"I didn't say that, dearest," John said quickly. "I just think it's the best thing. This man is a killer and he's sworn to get you. Even with a bodyguard, it's not going to be pleasant wondering if he's going to show up. Can't you see that, dear?"

"No," she said angrily. "What I do see is that you'd like me to leave town so I won't mess up your sweet little life." She hung up.

She was contrite a moment later. Of course he was right. What kind of date could they have, with a detective shadowing him and one watching her and newsmen following her to see if the prowler would show up. There would be absolutely no privacy. She flushed a deep red as she remembered Harry Plover. The detective had probably heard the entire conversation. She had been so relieved to hear John's voice that she had forgotten his presence in the house.

The remainder of the day passed quietly. At five Vita spoke to Unce Fred and then her mother, assuring the sick woman that the police had caught the prowler.

104

ALICE TOHMAS cheered her considerably by coming by half an hour later. She carried a bag full of groceries.

"I thought we might knock something together," she said. At that moment Blowston came out of the kitchen. "I didn't know you had company," he said apologetically.

"Well, I think we can cut the steaks so we can get three portions," Alice said a little doubtfully.

The detective grinned. "I love steak."

"What about Mr. Plover?" Vita asked.

"Oh he'll be relieved in half an hour. He'll go home to dinner."

Vita wished the detective would leave them alone for a few minutes. Alice had the same thought a moment later.

"Let's go into the bedroom, dear. I want to try that dress you promised me." She smiled at the red-faced detective and took Vita with her.

"Boy he's a creep," Alice said when they were inside. "How did you get him?" She started laughing and Vita found herself joining in.

"Isn't life fantastic?" Alice said. "You ever dream you were going to be front-paged in every paper in Los Angeles, your story told on a dozen television programs, newspaper photographers chasing you and six-foot detectives guarding your beautiful body?"

"No. Not in a million years."

"Doesn't it all seem a little unreal?" Alice asked.

Vita nodded. "I feel like I'm acting in a movie. I'm still not used to it. I mean knowing someone's listening in on your phone all the time. No, I think I'd enjoy it except for knowing some maniac's out to get me. Unless they've got him."

She told her about the man they had picked up. She started to tell Alice about Herbert, but changed her mind.

"How are things in the office?" Vita asked.

"Claire's trying to take over your job," Alice said. "But don't worry. She's too small to fit into your britches. Come on, I'm hungry. Let's eat."

They spent the next two hours preparing and eating dinner and Joe Blowston told them he hadn't had an assignment that good in years. He added he hoped it would last a while now he knew how good the cooking was and how pretty her friends were. He apologized lamely when he saw the look on the girls' faces.

The evening went smoothly. A tall man named Oscar Crandall replaced Harry Plover and disappeared into the kitchen where the monitoring telephone was installed.

Farley called at nine o'clock to say that the man they had picked up had confessed.

Vita was overjoyed. "Are you sure?" she cried.

"Positive. I just left him. We've been working on him all day and about an hour ago he finally broke down and admitted everything. Then we took down his statement. What really did it was the boy friend of that poor kid he strangled yesterday.

"The boy caught a glimpse of him as he ran past him in the dark. After he made an identification, we kept hammering away at the guy until he owned up."

"Who was he?" Vita asked.

"Oh some unemployed mechanic. He's got a list of sex offenses as long as your arm. Peeping into girls' dormitories, molesting children, self-exposure, everything except rape. And we caught him in the act. At first he tried to pretend he hadn't been in the neighborhood last week, but we broke that down. Goldberg can be a pretty good questioner when he wants to be."

"I think that's wonderful," she said. Suddenly the room looked twice as cheerful to her and she smiled at Alice and the detective. "Well I guess you feel wonderful too. Knowing this guy isn't on the loose."

"You're so right," she said gratefully.

"Let me talk to Blowston and I'll get those boys out of there. I'll bet they've been ruining your carpets dropping ashes all over the place."

She gave the phone to Blowston. A few minutes later the two detectives said good night and left.

"Do you want me to stay with you tonight," Alice asked.

"No, I think I'll be okay. All I need is some sleep."

"Good. See you in the office tomorrow."

A few minutes later Herbert Buhler called. Despite herself, Vita could not avoid a quick sense of fear when she heard his voice.

"Vita," he said, "I've got to talk to you. Can I come by?"

She hesitated. Farley's call had cleared her doubts about

106

him, but the feeling that he had suddenly become a stranger persisted.

"I was just about to take a bath and go to bed," she said at last, trying to make her tone as casual as possible. She did not want to hurt his feelings.

"Well, you go and take your bath. I just want to talk to you for a few minutes. It's been on my mind all day. I tried to get you before but couldn't."

"I'd rather let it wait till tomorrow, Herbert. Unless it's something terribly important. Can't it wait till then? I'm awfully tired."

"I'm sorry, Vita. It can't wait. I won't be here tomorrow," Herbert said.

"Where are you going?" Vita asked.

"I don't want to talk about it over the phone, Vita. I wanted to see you before I left and explain. Well, I guess it doesn't matter. After talking to my father I don't really care."

The disappointment in his voice was so sincere, she could not help a feeling of pity. She remembered what her Uncle Fred had said about Herbert's father's anger. He had probably given Herbert a hard time on the phone.

"I'm sorry, Herbert. I didn't mean to sound unfriendly. It's just that I'm very tired. After everything that happened. But I'll be glad to see you for a little while."

"Oh, thank you, Vita." The relief in his voice was obvious. "You take your bath. I'll be by in half an hour."

After he hung up, Vita could not help thinking of the resemblance between Herbert's voice and the prowler's. No, she thought, not quite the same but similar, as if one had been a distortion of the other.

After she finished her conversation with Herbert, Vita drew a tub of hot water, filled it with pink bath salts and soaked deliciously in them. Twice the telephone rang, but she paid no attention. Farley's news had removed all her anxiety. She found herself smiling as she thought of how she would have shuddered at hearing the telephone ring only a few hours earlier.

She changed into a soft blue gingham dress her mother had sent her and waited for Herbert. He came half an hour after he had called, as he had promised. She was a little shocked at his appearance. His eyes were red-rimmed as if he had not slept for days and his face had an unhealthy pallor.

"You look terrible, Herbert," she said. "Let me get you some tea."

"Thanks," he said, strangely quiet. She had never seen him

107

in such a mood before and she felt a little sorry for him.

"What's been happening to you?" she asked when they were having the tea a few minutes later. She knew it was a hypocritical question, but she could not simply ignore his complete dejection.

"Everything," he said. "My father practically threatened to disown me because of the story in the papers. And then I've had trouble at the school. Some mother sent in a complaint about me. Worst of all, I've been feeling terrible about what happened here that night."

In Goldberg's office, a nervous-looking blond young man sat staring at the window. Goldberg and Farley stood a few feet away watching him.

"You were caught peeping into a bedroom. Right?" Farley asked.

"Yes," the young man said tonelessly.

"How many times have you been picked up?" Goldberg asked.

"I don't know—nine or ten, I think," the man said.

"Why did you kill Carol Forsythe?" Goldberg said suddenly.

"I didn't kill anybody," the nervous young man said.

"You jumped her when she had her bathing suit down and started mauling her," Farley said. "When she started yelling you throttled her."

"No," the man said. "I swear I never went near that house."

"We know you were in the area when it happened. You admitted yourself you get dizzy spells and don't know what you're doing when you start peeping or showing yourself."

"I know," the youth said, crying. "I know, but I never killed anyone. I swear it."

"You never molested a girl? Never tried to rape or attack anyone sexually?" Goldberg said. "Don't lie because we'll check the record."

The youth hesitated. "Once, but I didn't kill anyone."

"What happened?" Goldberg pressed.

The young man swallowed hard. "About a month ago, I was walking in one of the parks and I noticed a boy and a girl making love."

"Go on," Goldberg said carefully. "Tell us what you did."

"I—I kind of lost my head. I got dizzy. I saw the girl lying there with her dress up. I always get dizzy when I see a girl naked."

"What happened?" Farley asked.

"I frightened the boy I guess. He was only about sixteen. He ran away and I fell on the ground near the girl and started playing with her."

"How? Did you penetrate her?" Goldberg said.

"No," the youth said. "No, I swear I didn't. I touched her there with my fingers. Just touched her between the legs. Then she started yelling and I hit her."

Goldberg and Farley exchanged quick glances.

"You don't like to get inside girls, Robert?" Goldberg asked gently. "Don't be afraid to answer. We know it's not your fault."

"No," the boy said. "I just want to see how they're made and play with them."

"You ever see a baby sitter by the name of Theresa Drury?" Goldberg asked softly.

"I don't think so," the boy said.

"You admit you get dizzy and you don't know what happens afterward sometimes, that right?" Farley said.

The youth nodded, still weeping.

"And it could happen that when you play with these girls and they scare you, you maybe choke them a little to stop them, don't you? I mean without knowing it even. Maybe not even wanting to?" Goldberg's voice, experienced with sex offense suspects, sounded extremely gentle.

"All you want is to look under their dresses or touch them on the outside and they get scared. Then you don't remember too well?"

The youth began to sob and nod his head.

"Do you remember calling any girls and making a little dirty talk," Goldberg asked. "You know, telling them you want to see their private parts and touch them?"

"I don't know," the boy sobbed.

"Call Vita and let her listen to him," Goldberg said suddenly. . . .

The telephone rang suddenly in Vita's living room. It was Lieutenant Goldberg.

"Vita, I'm sorry to disturb you. But something's come up. As Sergeant Farley told you we have a full confession to all the crimes by this man we picked up—Henderson. After we confronted him with the boy friend of the girl, he broke down. The boy friend has just called us and said he's not sure any more—it was too dark in the alley."

"But you said he confessed everything," Vita said. She could see Herbert looking at her with curiosity.

109

"I know, but he's a psychopath, Vita. These guys sometimes crack under too much questioning and admit anything. We plan to hold him anyway for the peeping offense. And we can check on all his alibis for the times the killings were done. But I wish you'd do something for me now."

"What?" Vita said. Herbert looked at her carefully.

"Do you think you'd remember the prowler's voice well enough to recognize it. I mean could you identify it?"

"I think so, yes."

"All right, I'm going to ask this guy to repeat a few of the words the prowler said to you. You listen carefully and tell me what you think. You don't mind doing this, do you?"

"No, of course not."

"Okay, here's Henderson."

A new voice came on. It was a tenor voice, and he repeated several sentences slowly, the same sentences the prowler had used. As she listened, Vita felt a chill enter her heart. It was a voice she had never heard in her life. Goldberg came on suddenly.

"Well?"

"It's not his voice, Lieutenant."

"Are you sure?" Goldberg asked.

"I'm positive," Vita said. She tried to avoid Herbert's eyes. He was looking at her thoughtfully.

"Gee, kid, I'm sorry. This guy seemed to fit everything we knew about him. I guess we'd better send Joe back to the house. Any calls come in from the prowler or someone who might be him."

"No," Vita said slowly.

"How about Herbert Buhler. He call?"

Vita felt her heart beating faster and faster as she looked up at Herbert, sitting a few feet away.

"Did Buhler call?" Goldberg repeated. "I'm sorry we called off the stake-out on him. If he calls you or tries to see you before Blowston gets there, let us know will you?"

"Yes," Vita said, almost hoarsely.

"What's the matter, kid?" Goldberg asked. "Anything wrong? Don't you feel well?"

Vita said nothing.

"Is anyone there with you?"

"Yes." She could feel her heart beating faster and hoped Herbert could not notice her fear.

"Buhler?"

"Yes."

"Is he acting funny?"

"I don't know." She hesitated. "I think so."

"Look I'll be right down in about fifteen minutes. Just act normal. Nonchalant. Don't excite him in any way and don't contradict him. And one more thing. If he lays a hand on you—don't scream or act terrified. You understand. Don't let him see any sign of fear. It might set him off. Now control yourself very carefully. Do you understand, Vita?"

"Yes," she said softly. Herbert was scowling at her now.

"Now hang up and tell him the police have called off the search."

She hung up slowly and faced Herbert.

"What was that all about?" he asked. "The police still bothering you?"

"They just wanted to tell me they called off the search," she said, trying to sound as casual as possible.

"Well, that's a surprise. Why? Have they found the man?"

"Yes, I guess so." She nodded toward the teapot. "More tea?"

"Yes, thanks." She poured him another cup.

He drank it slowly, his face wearing an expression of complete gloom.

Watching his dark look, Vita found herself unable to control an imperceptible quickening of her heartbeat. She hoped he could not hear it, or notice the breathiness in her voice.

"What's the matter with you?" Herbert said sharply.

His voice sounded like the crack of a pistol and she jumped.

"Nothing," she said. "Nothing at all."

"You look very tired," he said. "I'm sorry I had to come by. But I had to see you." He drew closer to her on the sofa and she could not avoid trembling.

"You're trembling," he said. He took her hand between his own and rubbed them. "You've had a hard time."

She sat absolutely still with a frozen smile on her face.

"That's why I came by. I'm sorry about that fracas the other night. I guess I acted like a fool. I wanted to tell you before. I even wanted to come to see you in the hospital, but the police wouldn't leave me alone. Do you know they've actually been following me around. And breaking into my desk. Do you know anything about that?"

"No," Vita said almost soundlessly. The touch of his fingers on her arm was giving her goose pimples. She fought an urge to move away. He stared woodenly at her.

"Anyway I'm leaving. The principal gave me quite a lecture on account of that newspaper story and the police snooping around. Then my father called. He practically threatened to send the marines after me if I didn't come home. He wants me to go to Europe for six months and then work in the bank." He sighed. "And the way I feel I can't turn it down. I don't want to stay in this town anyhow. I hate it. I hate the phoniness of the people, the fast, immoral tempo everybody lives by and the horrible emphasis on sex."

He put her hand down and glowered at her. "That's all they think about in this town. It's another Sodom, Vita." His voice was loud with bitterness and anger. "The women dress so provocatively they almost invite men to have evil lustful thoughts about them. No wonder there are so many sex crimes in this city. And you find it everywhere. Even in my own classes, the girls come to school dressed in a way that would make my poor mother turn over in her grave if she saw it."

He stood up angrily. "No, I tell you I'm glad to leave— glad to get the stink of this town out of my nostrils. At least where we come from people have some sense of decency. Women know how to keep themselves covered properly." He had worked himself up so much that his face was red and his eyes had widened till they seemed ready to jump out of their sockets. "And the terrible thing is, it's impossible to be decent, to keep yourself pure and Christian in the middle of Sodom. I remember even you once wore a bathing suit that was so revealing, I nearly died of shame." He looked at her so accusingly, she thought he was going to strike her. "Don't you know the kind of lust that creates?

"Why are you so pale," he asked suddenly. He sat down next to her and spoke more quietly. "I'm sorry. I promised myself not to get worked up about it any more and I didn't come here to talk about that, Vita." He paused and began again. "I wanted to ask you again if you'd marry me. We can both leave this horrible place. We could have our honeymoon in Europe and then settle down in Sioux City."

She looked at him, trying hard to say something, knowing that he expected an answer, but her lips seemed glued together. She could feel the sweat break out on her temples and her knees tremble.

"I guess I'm not the most romantic man in the world," Herbert said. "But I love you and I've never touched another woman. I swear that, Vita."

She smiled and tried to speak.

"Will you be mine, Vita? Will you make me the happiest man in the world?" Herbert said pleadingly. She could feel him growing more and more excited as he proposed to her.

"Yes," she said slowly trying to sound calm.

For a moment he stared at her unbelievingly, then he smiled, he put his arms around her suddenly, pressed her close and jammed his lips against hers.

An inchoate scream died in her throat as he pressed his face hungrily against hers. She shuddered and tried frantically to move away from him. Finally she broke away and stood up, staring at him with terror in her eyes.

"What's the matter?" he asked. "What's wrong?"

"Nothing," she said too loudly. "I'm just tired."

Herbert put his arm around her shoulder. But as he came closer she moved back quickly. "No," she said in panic. "No. Don't touch me!"

"But what's wrong," he repeated, confused. "You just said we would get married. What's the matter with you? I thought you loved me. Don't you?"

"Yes," she said remembering Goldberg's words. "Yes, I love you."

He came closer and took her in his arms. "I'm sorry I acted so quickly. I thought you wanted me to kiss you."

She began to sob hysterically, trembling in his arms.

"What's the matter, darling?" he asked. "What are you crying for?"

She was sobbing violently and shaking uncontrollably when the door was flung open and Lieutenant Goldberg, Farley and a uniformed officer entered. They saw Vita struggling to get out of Buhler's arms and ran forward. Goldberg and Farley leaped at Herbert and pulled him away from Vita while the officer covered him with a pistol. Herbert was speechless.

Before he could say anything, Farley had handcuffed him. Goldberg went to the sobbing girl and held her against his shoulder, speaking soothingly to her. "It's all right. It's all right, baby. You're safe. Calm down."

"He was trying to kill me," she cried. "I thought you'd never come." She began sobbing again, but not as violently as before.

"That's a lie," Herbert shouted incredulously. "I just asked her to marry me and she accepted." He looked at Vita. "Vita, tell them it's not true."

"He tried to kill me," was all she could say. "He tried to kill me."

"Take him into the car," Goldberg said. "I'll be out in a

minute." He took the terrified girl back to the sofa and made her lie down. Then he gave her a glass of water. "You'll be all right," he said soothingly. "Do you want someone to stay with you tonight? Or can we drop you at someone's house."

"No, I'll be all right," she said.

"I think you'd better stay with one of your girl friends tonight," he said in a kindly voice. "You shouldn't be alone. If you like you can come to my place. My wife can put you up in our daughter's room."

She smiled gratefully. "Thank you. But I think I can stay at my friend Alice's. Or she can come here."

A moment later she telephoned Alice, who agreed to spend the night with her. When she came with an overnight case later, the detective left. Vita saw him to the door.

"Tell me, Vita," he said softly. "Do you really feel now that Buhler is the man who called you."

She nodded. "When he started to talk to me and put his hands on me I had the feeling at once that it was him. There was no doubt in my mind any more. I realized I had never known him, that I was looking at a complete stranger. I was so paralyzed with fear I thought I was going to faint. I thought I would die if you hadn't got here soon."

Goldberg patted her hand. "You go in and go to bed. And forget about everything. It's all over."

When she returned to the living room Alice opened her case and removed a bottle of Scotch.

"You and I are going to have a drink, honey," she said. "Most of this is for you."

"I need it," Vita said. "I thought I'd die when he started yelling at me. The look in his eyes was the most horrible thing I've ever seen." She shook her head. "I just can't understand how I could know someone all my life and not really know anything about him."

19

HERBERT BUHLER at first angrily refused to answer any questions when he was taken to the station house. He accused Goldberg of persecuting him.

"You're trying to find a scapegoat," he said bitterly when he finally was brought into the detective's office. "I had nothing to do with it." He accused Vita of hysterical behavior.

"Do you deny you've been having relations with a fifteen-year-old girl in your class?" Goldberg asked.

"Of course I do," Herbert yelled.

"Okay, Buhler," Goldberg said. "Hold your horses. We'll check all your statements tomorrow as to your whereabouts. And we'll have the girl here to confront you with what she told us. You say that on the day the Forsythe girl was killed you were in the Hollywood library. And the night of the Gardenia killing you were in a church meeting. How about the fact that you weren't home for three hours after you left Vita's house the night we were there?"

"I was upset at seeing Palmer there and learning about that week-end trip," Herbert said. "And I wanted to forget it. So I did something I've never done in my life. I got drunk."

"Where?" Goldberg asked.

"I drove out to Long Beach." He gave them the approximate locations of three bars he had visited, but he could not remember all their names.

"Herbert," Goldberg said softly. "Don't you often get the feeling in class you want to reach out and play with the breasts and private parts of those young girls?"

Herbert flushed a deep red and said nothing.

"And when you get that feeling you try to fight it by punishing the girls, don't you?" Goldberg continued gently. "You give them lectures about the evils of sex, of sensuality, of lust. You hate them for it, don't you?"

"Yes," Herbert said heavily.

Goldberg said, "Tell me, Herbert, do you ever get dizzy spells or blackouts where you don't remember what happens for hours at a time?"

"No," Herbert said, looking, frightened, at his questioners.

"I think maybe you do, Herbert," Farley said. "And it may have been at those times that you did these things. Did you ever get arrested for any sex offenses? Did you ever get into sex parties when you were at school, for instance?"

"No."

"Are you sure," Farley persisted. "We can check, you know. If it happened anywhere in this country we'll know about it, so you'd better tell us."

"I—I did something once, but it wasn't my fault."

"What was it?" Goldberg asked.

"Once when I was in college, some frat brothers put a naked prostitute in my room and left her there. I was supposed to have relations with her for my initiation."

"Did you?" Farley asked.

"No. I tried. But I couldn't."

"You mean you were afraid to?" Goldberg asked.

"Yes," Herbert said miserably.

"Then what happened," Goldberg asked.

"Everybody at school knew about it and made fun of me."

Goldberg got up and sighed. "Okay, Herbert, we'll stop for now. Are you sure you don't want to confess to anything?"

"I haven't done anything," Herbert said.

"Okay, we'll talk again in the morning. You'll have to stay here."

"You mean you're arresting me?" Herbert asked incredulously.

"That's right." Goldberg said. "If I were you I'd call an attorney in the morning. Or we can do it for you, if you want."

"But I haven't done anything," Herbert protested.

"Vita says you were the one who called her those times, and she says you tried to attack her tonight," Goldberg said.

"She's mad," Herbert shouted. "She's just gotten over hysteria. How can you take the word of a hysterical girl?"

"She says it was a voice like yours, Herbert," Farley said quietly. "You probably spoke through a handkerchief, didn't you?"

"No, no," Herbert yelled. "I didn't call her. There are thousands of people who have voices like mine."

Goldberg nodded to a uniformed policeman to take Herbert.

"I'm not going to charge you with anything but assault right now. I want to check on those statements. But I still think you'd better get yourself a lawyer. Oh, by the way. Do you use a cigarette holder, Herbert?"

"I don't smoke," Herbert said coldly.

After Herbert left, Farley turned to his chief with admiration. "Where did you get that line about reaching out for the girls? He began to fall apart as soon as you started that."

"I've been grilling sex offenders in New York for ten years," Goldberg said. "It gets to be routine."

"What do you plan to do? Send for the girl's boy friend for an identification?"

"That and get the Green girl to confront him. That might break him."

Goldberg opened his desk and took out the assorted items he had picked up at the various places where the prowler had committed his crimes. There were a few cigarette stubs and

116

some pieces of cellophane. Also a few hairpins, advertising circulars and match books.

Goldberg fingered them for a minute absently. "There's something about Buhler that disturbs me."

"What?"

"He doesn't smoke. You know what I've been thinking is: why couldn't the prowler be some queer jerk who hangs around the neighborhood. They see him every day—he's part of the scenery. You know a guy with maybe odd little habits, but not too strange, not too conspicuous. You checked all that didn't you?"

"Sure I did," Farley said. "There are lots of oddballs in Hollywood. So why should that neighborhood be different. There's a postman who's a bug on fertilizer. Reads about it all the time and makes his own mixtures. Talks about the best manure for roses, the best compost for gladiolas, and so on. There's a newsboy who sucks a lollipop all day while he delivers those throwaway newspapers like the *Hollywood Advertiser*. Never takes the thing out of his mouth. There's a guy delivers bread in a truck and he stutters in a Hungarian accent which makes most people laugh. There are also a couple of old men who are always drunk and there's a writer who keeps a couple of monkeys. A little odd, Abe, but that hardly makes them killers or sex criminals. Of course if you want me to round them up I will. It could be the writer—they're all a little nuts anyway."

Goldberg shook his head. "No. That wouldn't do any good. Too many. If there were only something about one of them we could tie up with what we know about the prowler. There must be something."

"Like a guy who uses a cigarette holder. That might be a lead. Men don't use them too much any more. Not here anyway. And if he did, he might just be a pansy."

Goldberg thought for a minute. "The kid didn't say absolutely it was a cigarette holder, Jim. It was dark and he saw it from a distance. It could have been anything long—say a straw, a pencil. Some guys like to chew on pencils. I do it myself once in a while. Or it could even be something else."

Farley shook his head. "Abe," he said in a strange voice, "I've been holding something back on you."

Goldberg looked surprised. "Holding back what?"

The Irish detective stood up and shrugged. "I don't know —maybe I'm just jumpy. Maybe there's nothing in it." He took the plunge. "It's about my nephew."

"Tony?" Goldberg asked. "What's he done now?"

Farley repeated a conversation he had had with the boy. His big face flushed with embarrassment.

"For Christ sake, Jim," Goldberg said, "so what? A thousand guys wander around aimlessly and don't remember where they've been."

"I know," Farley said miserably. "But Tony's sick." He hated to use the word, but he spit it out now. "He's a psychoneurotic. He doesn't know why he wanders around. Like that time he was picked up."

Goldberg snorted. "Jim, you're crazy. Tony couldn't do anything like this. He's a mixed-up kid, that's all. You ought to be ashamed even thinking a thing like that."

"I just thought I ought to tell you," Farley said. He sat down heavily near the desk. "It's been on my mind all day."

Goldberg looked sympathetic. "Jim, you better ease off. Why don't you go out and have a few belts, forget the case for a couple of hours."

"Yeah," Farley said. "I guess I should be ashamed. There was a catch in his voice when he continued. "I think if it ever were Tony, I'd go off my rocker. I love that kid more than anything in the world." He stood up. "Want to have a belt with me?"

"No, I'd better get home. Becky's getting sore about my never getting home. You're lucky you're not married. When I quit this case, I'm going to be a cigar maker. They get home nights."

Becky Goldberg was dozing on their bed when he entered. She had obviously intended waiting up for him and had fallen asleep with the light on. The afternoon papers, loud with sex-crime headlines, was on the nighttable. Her dark, thin face seemed younger on the white pillow. She lay in her slip, which had twisted slightly under her. Goldberg studied his wife's worn face quietly, reluctant to disturb her sleep. A feeling of tenderness, mixed with pity and desire, filled him as he watched her mature breasts rise and fall gently. He could not help noticing the runs in her stockings or the faded pink of her slip, which had seen too many washings. He reminded himself guiltily that he had forgotten to pick up her watch for the third day.

He bent over her and pressed his lips affectionately to her shoulder and then to the cleft of her bosom. Becky stirred and opened her eyes as she felt his lips. He felt her stiffen and turn away. The gesture of rejection pained him. He put an arm around her and kissed her warmly on the mouth.

"I'm sorry I'm so late, honey," he said. "Still on that case."

"That damned case," she said wearily. She barely responded to his lips. She seemed almost alienated from him. He held her close. She started to get up. "I'll make you a sandwich and some coffee."

"No," he said, holding her down. "I'm not hungry." Silently he began to caress the soft skin of her back and kissed her shoulder. His fingers strayed lightly over her breasts. He felt her body grow rigid, ungiving under his touch.

"Abe," she said hesitantly, moving away a little. "I don't feel like it tonight." She looked worriedly at him. "You don't mind, do you?"

"No," he lied. "I'm too tired anyhow." There was no use talking about it. He felt chagrined and frustrated as he removed his shirt. It was on the tip of his tongue to shout, "God damn it, did I attack those girls? Did I strangle them?" But he remained silent.

He waited for her to comment, but she simply stared at him. "What're you so sore about?" he asked finally. "I know the case's been hell on you. I know I never put in all this night work in New York. But who wanted to come to sunny California? Me?"

"Stop shouting, Abe, I can hear you. I'm not sore about anything. Not about the case anyhow," she added bitterly.

He stepped into his pajamas. "Then what? Oh, I forgot the watch again."

"That's not all you forgot," Becky said, as she put on her nightgown.

"What else?"

"You forgot we were married twenty years ago today," Becky said quietly, putting out the light.

20

Alice waited until nine o'clock the next morning before she called Helen Wright to say she was not coming in.

"I know Helen," she told Vita as they finished their third cup of breakfast coffee. "If I called her at home before she left, she'd start screaming that the work couldn't get done."

Helen screamed anyway. "You've got to come in," she wailed. "I'm all alone. Vita's out and Claire's just called to say she's sick. I don't know what's happened to her. She sounded absolutely awful when I talked with her. Everything's gone wrong. Mr. Dennison called this morning to say I couldn't possibly go to Europe this year."

"No!" Alice said amazed. "He can't do that. You had your reservations and made advance payment for the hotel rooms. Didn't you tell him that, for Pete's sake?"

"It's no use," Helen shouted disconsolately. "I tried to beg him to change his mind, but he said he'd clean the whole section out if I left. He said he had just had enough. He's been screaming at me to get that presentation for the directors who are coming and I just can't do it alone. You've just got to come in, Alice, please!"

Alice frowned and told Helen to wait. She clamped her palm over the instrument. "She's having a tantrum. Claire's out too. She sounds like the place'll come down over her ears if I don't show up. And on top of everything that son-of-a-bitch Dennison cancelled her European trip."

Vita paled. "Oh, God, no! He can't. She's been dreaming of nothing else for three years. Tell her I'll do her work while she's gone."

"Don't be silly," Alice said. "Nothing ever changes that bastard's mind. I'll tell her I'll be in after lunch."

"No," Vita said, "you don't have to baby-sit with me. You can't leave her alone like that. You'd never be able to live with her afterward."

"Oh, hell," Alice said. "Helen doesn't scare me. She's just a damned worrier and Dennison makes her wet her pants whenever he yells."

"No, please, Alice." Vita begged. She felt terrible about Dennison's cancellation of Helen's trip and she did not want to be responsible for any further trouble at the office. She knew also that Alice had no money saved and needed her job. "I'll be okay. I've got some letters to write and then I think I'll drive out to the beach. Why don't you come back for supper?"

"Okay." She told Helen she would come in. "I think you'll be all right now that they have the bastard." She hesitated. "Have you seen John lately?"

"No," Vita said unhappily, "he's giving me a wide berth. Everybody is. Except you. And I suppose when Herbert's trial comes up and I have to testify it'll get worse. I'll have to go somewhere and hide."

"Good. I'll go with you. We can go to Mexico. I've about had it in Southern California. Maybe I can get a man in Mexico," Alice said bitterly.

"Well, I'm off. I'll bring us some steaks. Maybe they'll taste better without smelly detectives around. Though," she grinned, "I wouldn't mind having Farley. I thought he was going to ask me for a date yesterday. But he didn't."

"Farley?" Vita asked, surprised.

"Sure, he was dying to ask me. I can always tell. A man's Adam's apple begins to quiver in a certain way. But he didn't." She sighed. "That's been the story of my life in this damned town. The only men who ask me out are married and there's no future in that. Which I am not buying. But that's what happens when you're a spinster of thirty-five. It's a lonely life." She rose to go. "Well, forget about Farley. He'll never ask me. I'd have to ask him."

"I'm sorry, Alice," Vita said, pressing the girl's hand. "I had no idea you were so lonely. Maybe we can do things together." She felt concerned.

Alice laughed. "Don't worry about me. I'll get a man even if I have to advertise for one in the columns of the *Mirror*. Which," she added bitterly, "I'm close to doing. So long, kid. Be back early."

Vita read on the couch for an hour and listened to some music. After a while she began to repair one of her dresses. The music and the bright summer sunlight streaming through the windows made her feel better. She trembled involuntarily as she heard the sharp ring of the doorbell. "I'm still shaky," she told herself. She moved slowly to the door, feeling uneasiness as she swung it open. John Palmer smiled at her. She grinned with relief, but a second later her face fell. He had never looked so tired and beaten. He was unshaven, his eyes were slightly bloodshot and his starched white shirt was smudged at the collar. His blue pin-stripe suit looked as if he had slept in it.

"May I come in?" he asked softly.

She nodded, shocked by his unkept appearance and the look on his face. He made no attempt to kiss her as he walked past her. When he had sat down on the sofa, he grinned weakly.

"Have you had breakfast?" she asked, wondering nervously what he had come to tell her.

"No," he said. "But don't bother, please. I just wanted to talk to you."

"It's no bother." She looked worriedly at him. "Wouldn't

121

you like a bath? You look as if you've been up all night."

"I have. I've been wandering around all night," he said, smiling wanly.

"What on earth for?" she asked. "Has something happened I don't know about?"

"You happened," he said. "After I phoned you yesterday. After you hung up."

"Oh, forget that," she protested. "I was nervous and upset and I was sick of hearing everybody in Los Angeles tell me to pack up and leave town. Like a scared little girl. You just hit me at the wrong moment."

He shook his head. "It doesn't matter. You were right. I have been worried about my job and money. More than anything else. I've been rationalizing my fears ever since I knew I loved you simply because I was unable to face an unpleasant truth about myself."

She made a quick gesture with her hand that said, *No apologies are needed.*

"I'm not doing this just to apologize, baby," John said. "And don't shut me up. I've been building up to this for hours. It was something I had to face up to for my own sweet good. Even if you turned me down cold and God knows you have every right."

He bridged his eyes tiredly with his hand and sat down on the couch.

"It finally happened. I saw myself for exactly what I was—just another slick Madison Avenue jerk in a gray flannel suit. Just like your friend Herbert said. As a matter of fact I think I owe him an apology. I hated his guts and I hated his pompous, smug, Babbitt-like self-righteousness. I hated them all even more because he went out with you and kept drawing you into that pure, one-hundred per cent Presbyterian world into which a spoiled Methodist like me could never hope to enter."

"Stop it, John, stop it," she said. His bitterness was more than she could stand. "Please don't hurt yourself that way. It wasn't your fault. You were married before I ever met you and you worked long and hard to get that job at Stevens. There are very few people who wouldn't have acted as you did."

"I called Ginny a few minutes ago," John interrupted, "and told her she could have the divorce on her terms. She gets the house, the car, the stocks, bonds, everything except some pin money. Enough to buy me hamburgers till I can find work."

122

"Work? You mean you're quitting Stevens?" she asked.

"Sure, that's one of her terms: I have to get out of Los Angeles. She's not going to have her friends watch me get married to another girl I've left her for—whether it's you or anyone else. Pride like Ginny's has no equal. That was one of her terms and the one she counted on most to keep me in harness." He sighed. "I won't kid you. It's not going to be easy giving up that money, or that job."

She kissed him impulsively, pressing her face against the hard scratchy stubble of his beard. For a moment she could not trust herself to speak. Then she smiled and said, "You go in there and shower and shave. And when you come out I'll have breakfast for you. Bacon and eggs, juice, coffee and hot bread. Sound all right?"

He nodded. "How do you feel about marrying a bum with just enough money to keep us in franks and beans for the next few months?"

"I love franks and beans," she said. "Get out of here. You really do look like a bum. You can change that shirt. I still have one of your sport shirts in the closet." She slapped his rear as he rose, laughing.

She could hear him singing in the shower a moment later. But when he sat down to eat, he was apprehensive again.

"How about your mother? How's she going to take you're marrying a divorced man?"

"I think it's about time my mother was weaned," Vita said firmly. "You know I've realized an important truth about *myself* these last few days. I'm a worrier. I worry about everything. My mother, my job, my love life. And a large part of it is due to the fact that I've never let myself make an important decision without worrying first how my mother would take it."

She poured second cups of coffee for them. "I realized I couldn't do that any more after I got out of the hospital and everybody kept telling me to leave town. I was almost scared enough to do it too. But something stopped me. And after I stopped, I knew I'd have to stop worrying about what people like my mother or Helen Wright or Herbert Buhler think."

"Well, that's one thing we can thank the prowler for," he said thoughtfully. "None of this might have happened to us if he hadn't kicked over the traces. You might have gone on tied to the silver cord and I might have gone on trying to protect my beautiful twelve-room house and Cadillac. It's an ill wind that blows no good, as Shakespeare said." He laughed.

"Christ, I'm just lousy with quotes today. Whenever I get self-analytical I get cultured as hell. Hit me with the sugar bowl if I try any more."

"There's something I'd better tell you about Herbert," she said very seriously.

"Don't say it. I made an ass of myself hitting him and I'm sorry. That was another thing I wanted to say. I guess I acted out of childish jealousy."

She shook her head and told him about Herbert's visit, his arrest and what Farley had said about him. John was astounded.

"Him? The prowler? It's impossible. The guy's a meatball, sure, but he couldn't hurt a fly."

"What makes you so sure?" she said. "I know the prowler sounded like him—and how about all those things he said and did?"

"Vita, you were scared stiff by the prowler. A hundred guys could sound like Herbert, especially if they come from your neck of the woods. As for the school business—well it fits in with his conflicts about sex and his guilt feelings. And if he kissed you and asked you to marry him— Well, the guy was nuts about you, you know that."

Vita looked at him. "Maybe you're right. But I'm still not sure, John. You didn't see the way he looked at me yesterday."

John kissed her hand tenderly. "I think we both need a change of pace. I'm going to my lawyers' with Ginny this afternoon and sign an agreement. After that we can leave town. I can get a divorce in Juarez, Mexico and we can drive to New York after we're married. That is, if we can use your car."

"We sure can," she smiled.

"We're going to be happy, darling," he said. "I'm not the easiest guy in the world to live with. But I'll make you laugh. I could kick myself for hanging on all these months. I must have been out of my head. How could I, knowing anybody as wonderful as you?"

"I love you," she said slowly, studying his face, "I love you and that's big enough to soak up your pain as well as mine. For a while I wanted to break away myself. I felt hurt and small and completely unimportant. I felt that way when you called last time. But after I hung up I realized I was acting like a neurotic, demanding that everything be molded to fit my own needs. I knew that wasn't love. Love doesn't force a situation. It may turn away because it knows it cannot win—" She stopped. "I've been frightened about too many things all my life—of my mother, physical love, even of myself. When I started getting frightened because I loved you and it wasn't going well, I decided it was too damned much."

He crushed her to him in a wave of tenderness and for a moment, he could not trust himself to speak. "We're going to be good together. I feel it in my bones. I'd better jump now. I'll be back the minute this damned inquisition is over and we'll have a drink to celebrate. Do you think you can get away tonight or tomorrow?" he asked suddenly. "I mean, don't they need you here? The police I mean?"

"I don't see why," she said firmly. "If they want me for any court testimony I can always come back, I suppose, though I hope to God I won't have to." She took his hands. "Let's go as soon as we can."

He laughed, pleased. "Done. We can drive to Mexico. It'll take me about a week to get a decree and we can keep from getting bored by going to the bullfights. They've got a great ring in Juarez."

John was suddenly serious. He hesitated. "I don't want to scare you any more, darling. But if Buhler is not the prowler, then the real one is still around. And you're on his list."

She paled a little. "I'll be careful. Please hurry back, darling."

It was only after John sat behind the wheel that he remembered the Forsythe girl was strangled in broad daylight. He started to get out of the car to warn Vita to go to a movie or see a friend, but decided not to. He should be back fairly soon and he was reluctant to add to her jitters. She had been through too much already.

21

When Carlotta Green strolled through the lobby of the police station, she nearly stopped traffic. Several patrolmen, bail bondsmen and even a policewoman turned to stare at the tall, dark fifteen-year-old whose breasts and hips seemed ready to burst from her skin-tight red sheath. Flanked by her mother and an attorney, Carlotta moved majestically down the hall, pleasantly aware of male eyes on her shapely breasts and legs. So long as they stared, she felt completely secure. Male sexual interest was a heady wine to her.

It was only when Lieutenant Goldberg began to ask her questions in a bored, indifferent voice that seemed to black out her sex, that she began to feel uneasy. The detective's grave, probing voice reminded her of the catechismal drone of the priests in church. She listened unhappily while Goldberg outlined what they knew about her and Buhler. She felt like a small child who was being scolded by an elder.

"I want you to tell it to him, straight to his face, Carlotta," Goldberg explained carefully. "We're counting on you to break him down. We still have no certain evidence that he is the prowler. We're checking that and a psychiatrist will examine him later. But it's been my own experience in New York that sometimes the most hardened sex criminal will break down when he's accused face to face by his victim." He stopped and looked kindly at the girl. "I know it's not a pleasant experience, Carlotta, and I'm sorry to put you through it. But it won't take too long. He's already been identified by someone else as the prowler. The shock of having you confront him this way should knock him off his pins completely."

He looked at Carlotta's mother, a tall, good-looking blonde in her late thirties. Mrs. Green moved a carefully manicured hand lightly over her new pageboy fluff and nodded. The attorney, a serious-looking short man with a large nose that held rimless glasses, bowed in agreement.

"Do I have to say it to his face?" Carlotta asked.

"Just like you told it to me at the house an hour ago," Farley said from the other side of the room.

"Get him in here," Goldberg told Farley. A moment later Herbert Buhler was brought in. He looked pale, as if he'd had no sleep, his blue eyes seemed to be on fire as he stared at the girl and the people around her. Mrs. Green favored him with a look of contempt and loathing.

"Is this the man?" Goldberg asked without preliminaries. Carlotta looked at Buhler and flushed. She nodded, staring at the floor. Goldberg looked at her and began.

"All right, Buhler. Carlotta has told us all about it. She says you picked her up after school and took her up to your apartment. You gave her some bourbon and told her you were crazy about her. That you couldn't stand being near her any more, that you couldn't do any work while she was in your class because of your excitement. She also said you kept her after class and put your hand up her skirt.

"After she drank some whisky, you tried to get her to take off her clothes, but she wouldn't. So you chased her around the room. You offered her money, but she turned it down. Then you told her you'd flunk her and you started acting wild, getting excited and threw her on the couch and started tearing at her skirt. She got panicky and thought you were going to rape her or kill her and she took off her clothes. You kept her there naked for two hours doing all sorts of things that I won't even mention to spare her and her mother."

While he talked Carlotta looked carefully away from both Buhler and the detective. Her mother fastened her eyes grimly to Buhler's. Herbert stood listening stonily.

"I don't think we have to go on," Goldberg said, watching Buhler. "You can't stand being near young women or girls without feeling an urge to attack them and sometimes, when the urge is uncontrollable, you black out and you assault them the way you did Vita last night. Usually you get carried away so much, you don't even remember you've killed them. I think maybe you can tell us about that now, Buhler."

Buhler stared at the girl and said nothing.

"Do you deny what the girl told us? Do you deny you took her home and molested her?"

"I never layed hands on her," Buhler said stressing each word.

"You never layed hands on her? What did you do when you kept her in your place two hours, play chess?"

"I never took her home or any place. I never touched her," Buhler repeated slowly, still staring at the girl.

Goldberg looked annoyed. "Carlotta, did this man take you home and force you to submit to him?"

Carlotta hesitated. Her mother put her arm around the girl. "Speak up, honey. Don't worry, he can't hurt you."

Carlotta looked at Goldberg and said "yes," in a low voice.

"It's a dirty lie!" Buhler shouted at her. "You know it's a lie, Carlotta. Look at me. I dare you to look at me while I'm talking and say that I layed a hand on you."

Carlotta turned away from him. The attorney cleared his throat. "I think that's all we need, Lieutenant?"

"No, it isn't," Buhler shouted. "I know the law. I have the right to be confronted by my own accuser."

"You'll have that right in a court of law," the attorney snapped.

"I want it now," Buhler said turning to Goldberg. "I've been accused of committing a disgusting, loathsome offense.

And all I'm asking is that she look at me and deny what I have to say to her. Is that too much to ask?"

"Go ahead," Goldberg said. "Make it fast."

"I never touched you in my life," Buhler said looking at Carlotta. "I admit I've had lustful thoughts about you when you sat in front of me. But I've done my penance in prayer for them afterwards. I know that I am a sinner and that I must cleanse myself. But I swear before God Almighty that I never laid a hand on you. Never touched your flesh, nor took you to my house. I dare you to look me in the eye and say that is not the truth."

Carlotta kept her eyes fastened to the ground.

"Look at me!" Herbert thundered. "Look me in the eyes and accuse me of those things. May God strike me dead if I did any one of them." He turned to the detectives. "She concocted the whole story to destroy me. She sat there day after day, tempting me, hating me because I refused to give in to my lust."

Carlotta raised her eyes slowly and stared at Buhler. She began to tremble and moved closer to her mother.

"You slimy bastard," Mrs. Green said, putting her arm protectively about Carlotta, "you pervert. I ought to kill you."

"Wait a minute," Goldberg said quietly, "answer him, Carlotta."

Carlotta stood absolutely still, her lips pressed tightly together.

"Is what he says true?" Goldberg said. "Speak up."

"I really don't think," the attorney began weakly, but Goldberg motioned him to be quiet.

"Did you make that story up?" Goldberg asked in a hard voice. "Do you realize what can happen to this man if you're lying?"

Carlotta watched him silently. Everyone stared at her. A flush suffused her mother's face as she looked at her daughter. Suddenly, without warning, she slapped the child hard twice on the cheek. Carlotta did not flinch.

Goldberg sighed. "Take him back, Jim."

"Are you letting me go?" Herbert said.

"Not yet," Goldberg said. "We're still checking that alibi of yours. And I want you to talk to the psychiatrist. But if you're clean, you'll be released this afternoon."

Buhler marched out of the office without another look at Carlotta or her mother. The fifteen-year-old girl stood white-faced next to Mrs. Green.

128

"It's my own fault," Mrs. Green said slowly, as if she were speaking to herself. "I've been too busy getting married or divorced. I always thought I'd have plenty of time for her later." She looked at the girl. "She always seemed so little. And she's grown up so fast."

The detectives watched the mother and daughter leave silently. Goldberg sat at his desk staring at the opposite wall for a moment, unable to say anything. Farley looked at him sympathetically. He knew how the older man felt. If you worked hard enough on a case, it was maddening sitting around watching it fall apart. He wished he could say something to console his chief.

Goldberg banged his fist on the table suddenly and turned his bloodshot, sleepless eyes on Farley.

"I don't give a Goddamn what that little bitch said. Buhler's nuts in the sex department. I've talked to these bastards for years. I can smell them a block away. I've seen a dozen guys like Buhler involved in sex crimes in New York. Mild, harmless-looking men who look as if they did nothing but collect stamps or butterflies."

Farley listened silently, unwilling to support or oppose his chief's words. If he fed Goldberg's fire now, it would be harder to quench later. He was beginning to realize how much the strain was affecting the other man and wondered if he were starting to crack.

"Well we'll know more when the psychiatrist gets through with him," Goldberg said softly, as if to convince himself.

22

Vita had finished packing her suitcases by two o'clock and felt tired. She lowered the blinds and locked the front door and lay down on the living-room sofa to take a nap. She had called the office and Alice told her that Helen Wright was in Pasadena at the photographers' and would not be back till three. Alice was delighted with Vita's news.

Vita had removed her dress in order not to wrinkle it and made herself comfortable on the long sofa, adjusting the soft pillows under her head. She thought for several minutes of the conversation with John and hoped the lawyer's meeting would not be too painful. It seemed to her that she had barely dozed off when she heard footsteps in the kitchen. She raised her head a little but decided she was wrong. A moment later she heard another noise and looked at the ceiling. Perhaps her landlord had returned a little early and was moving down the back stairs. She closed her eyes again. A few seconds later she heard footsteps coming into the living room and opened her eyes quickly.

She was surprised to see Mr. Alger, the newsboy, standing there with a lollipop in his mouth and the canvas bag of papers around his neck. Vita sat up and stared at him. He had never come in the house before. She blushed as she remembered she was in her slip.

"Oh, I'm sorry, Mr. Alger," she said. "I fell asleep. It's nice of you to bring the paper inside."

He grinned and gave her a copy. "I found the door open so I came in. You looked real pretty, lying there asleep. I almost hated to disturb you," he said, smiling in his gentle fashion. "You feeling all right now, Vita?" He kept sucking on the lollipop.

She looked at him surprised. He had never addressed her by her first name before. "Well, I'm still a little tired, Mr. Alger." She was obscurely irritated by his coming into the house without knocking. I've probably given him reason to think it's all right because I talk to him so much.

Mr. Alger bit into the hard candy at the end of the stick and chewed it. The noise of his teeth crunching the candy disgusted her. She wondered what she could say to get him to leave. She did not dislike the young man and always responded to his greetings, but she thought him a little stupid. Besides it was almost three and she wanted to call Helen.

Mr. Alger took a fresh lollipop wrapped in cellophane from the chest pocket of the dirty gray dungarees he wore and held it out to her. "Raspberry," he said.

"No thanks, Mr. Alger," she said, "I just had my lunch and I'm not hungry." She hesitated and said, "If you'll excuse me, I've got to make an important telephone call. You see I'm leaving town tonight."

He looked strangely at her. "I'm very sorry to hear that, Vita. Very sorry. Where you going?"

"Well, I'm getting married, actually," she said, wishing he would leave. "Well, thanks for bringing the paper, Mr. Alger and good luck to you." She turned her back to him as a strong hint and dialed the number of the office. A few seconds later she asked for Helen's extension. It was busy and the operator asked her if she wished to hang on. She said yes and waited. She remembered hearing no sound of his leaving and turned around. Mr. Alger was still there. He had finished eating the lollipop candy and was breaking the stick in two with his dirty fingers, smudged from handling the freshly printed newspapers.

"I'm sorry," she said feeling a premonition that something was wrong. "Was there something else you wanted to say, Mr. Alger?"

"Not especially," he said, "you gò make your call. I can wait."

"Why should you wait?" she asked slowly, feeling a chill in her stomach.

"Well, you asked me to come here, Vita."

"I asked you?" she repeated staring at him.

"Sure. When I called you the other night. I told you I wanted to come by and you said you were too tired then. I tried to get you at the office and left a message. Yesterday you had company. I wanted to come when you were alone so I could see you."

"See me?" she said, unable to take her eyes away from his own piercing, blue ones.

"Like I asked you to," he said earnestly. He put his hand under her slip quickly and squeezed the warm flesh of her thighs. "I want to see you with nothing on."

She knew who it was then and only a lightning-like effort at self-control kept her from screaming or trying to flee. One gesture that would frighten him would mean her death. In the midst of her terror, a cool center of reason operated, like the eye of a hurricane, and it dictated every move, every word. She sat perfectly still, the phone glued to her ear, while he rolled back the hem of her slip and admired her thighs. When he swooped to kiss her neck, she could hear Helen Wright's prim voice saying "Hello, Helen Wright speaking."

Conscious of the wet warmth of his lips against her neck and a feeling of nausea in her stomach, she said weakly, "Hello, Helen."

"Is that you, Vita?" Helen said quickly.

Mr. Alger cupped Vita's breast and squeezed it. Vita trembled a little but did not move away or flinch.

"Vita," Helen repeated, "is that you?"

"Yes," Vita said weakly. "Helen I—" She could not continue with his lips slobbering on her neck and throat. Mr.

131

Alger took the phone gently from her hand and put it in its cradle. "Call her later," he said tenderly. "You can speak to her later."

He caressed her thighs. "They're so soft like silk. And yet they're so hard and strong." He squeezed the calf of her leg and then he raised his trouser leg. He put her hand on his calf. "See I'm as strong as you are there."

He reached for her hand and applied pressure till she winced. "I could squeeze your hand to a pulp, just while I'm sitting here talking to you. That's the kind of strength I have." He relaxed his grip and withdrew his hand. Her fingers felt numbed, paralyzed. He gave her a hard, glittery smile. "But I won't hurt you, Vita. I like you. I've liked you ever since I met you. You're kind and understanding. You always have time to talk to me. Not like some of that trash across the street who wouldn't be caught dead speaking to a newsboy who gives out free copies. You're different. I can always tell a lady.

"Before I took this job I used to stack cans for a supermarket in Hollywood," he said, "and the girls there—they were all dirty. I took them up to my room sometimes and loved them up a little. But I never got inside and that made them mad. I told them I hated *that place*. But I could always tell they were trash. You know how, Vita? Well when I took off their dresses I could see their underwear. You know those girls would be wearing brand new dresses—fresh off a Beverly Hills shop rack. But underneath their panties would be torn, or frayed or patched up. I can always tell a girl's a lady by her underwear." He lifted the hem of her slip high until he could see the white of her panties. "I can see you're a lady."

He looked at her carefully. "That guy you're going to marry. He's a lucky man. Couldn't find no better girl anywhere. Kind and gentle and understanding. And beautiful. I knew a girl like you in Indiana. I loved her. But she had too much school education for me. She used to talk to me for hours in the library where she worked. She was a nice girl. Really nice. It was too bad, what happened." He squeezed her breast. "You want to know what happened, Vita? That's why I came out here."

"What happened?" she asked obediently.

"I came to her house one night. I had asked her, oh, I guess a hundred times to let me go out with her. But she said no. So one night I got a bunch of flowers and went to see her. She acted like she was annoyed, and asked me to leave. I

132

said I just wanted to talk to her and see what she looked like in the places she hid from me. I rolled up her skirt and started looking underneath, when she started screaming. I couldn't help it then. My hands acted like they didn't even know they were mine." He put his hand under her slip and began tugging at her panties. "You're just like silk, there. She had a rougher skin, much rougher."

"Would you like some coffee and cake?" she asked. She was fighting for time. "I'd like it fine," he said, "and then we can take all your clothes off. I want to see you all naked, Vita. Okay?"

"Yes," she said slowly, "I'll just go to the kitchen and make some tea." Perhaps she could beckon to a neighbor or a passer-by, she thought wildly, anybody who could stop him before he tried to rape her.

"I'll get it," he said. "I'll put the tea to boil. You tell me where everything is. You stay here and rest. Don't move."

"But I know where everything is," she said. "It'll take too long." ·

"All right," he said a little petulantly. "Let's go and get it over with. I want to see you with nothing on."

The telephone rang a moment later, but she was afraid to answer it.

The tall, balding psychiatrist sat in the armchair next to Lieutenant Goldberg's desk and played with his gold pencil.

"I'm sorry to have taken so long, Lieutenant," he said. "But it was very slow going. He wouldn't open his mouth to say anything at first and then it was like pulling teeth for about two hours, when suddenly the dam burst and it all came out."

Goldberg nodded and looked at Farley. "What came out?"

The psychiatrist drew his palms together. "Buhler has got an Oedipus Complex, for one thing. I wouldn't want to swear to it after one interview, but it's definitely indicated. He was raised largely by his mother, who had always wanted a girl. She treated him like a girl and he wore skirts till he was five. Definite signs of traumatic disturbance connected with that, I think. Now I gather that his father at one time stopped having relations with his mother or they lived in separate rooms. Buhler seems to have a strong subconscious hostility to his father."

"Look, Doctor," Goldberg said a little impatiently. "All this is extremely interesting. But what we want to know is, could he have done these crimes? And did he give you anything that might indicate he did? We've got several murders to solve and we're trying to prevent more."

The psychiatrist nodded. "I don't think so. I don't honestly think so."

When he had left Goldberg turned disgustedly to Farley.

"Total score zero. The alibis check, the girl backtracked and now this egghead tells us he's just a harmless jerk who was scared of girls because his mother put him in skirts."

Goldberg took the transcript of the prowler's calls out of his desk and started reading it again, checking each of the prowler's sentences carefully. He shook his head. "I guess I was really counting on his opening up to the headshrinker at the last minute. Comes from seeing too many movies about psychoanalysts. You always see these eggheads jabbing a needle into these guys—then they lay on the couch and the guy says 'I did it!' We've come to believe those guys can work miracles. Maybe that's what we need here—a miracle."

"I don't put much stock in psychoanalysts. I pay one of them twenty dollars an hour. He lets my nephew pour his heart out and then says 'tsk tsk.' I told him he was a sucker. This doctor makes a fortune out of it. He specializes in kids. When one of these neurotic kids comes in, the analyst gives him a lollipop to suck on to make him feel better. The analyst says it makes the kid more co-operative."

Farley laughed. "I told Tony he ought to suck on one himself, maybe he'd have a better session. So he asked the analyst if it would work the same way with him. You know my nephew's kind of naive, and he takes everything people tell him seriously." Farley stopped as he saw Goldberg look at him fixedly. "I'm sorry, Abe. I didn't mean to run on. Want me to check the reports downstairs to see if we picked up anybody?"

"What did the analyst say to your nephew?" Goldberg asked suddenly.

"Oh, he told him it wouldn't work with a man because a lollipop is usually accepted as a childish symbol and it might just sort of backfire."

"In other words most grown men wouldn't go around sucking lollipops."

Farley stopped. "What are you getting at, Abe?"

Goldberg opened his desk and took out the small pieces of cellophane found near the murdered women. "Vita said she heard slurping and clicking noises over the phone."

"And those scraps," Farley said, "could have come from lollipops."

"They were right near the Forsythe girl's body," Goldberg said.

"Holy smoke," Farley said. "Then—"

"Let's pick up that newsboy right away. I want to talk to him. How can we check where he lives?"

"Call the *Hollywood Citizen* circulation department, I guess," Farley said. He started to dial information.

"Wait. Call Vita first and put her on her guard. They usually deliver those papers in the afternoon. Tell her to keep the door locked and then we'd better detail Joe to go down there in case he shows up."

Farley dialed Vita's number. There was no answer. He looked apprehensively at Goldberg.

"She may have gone to the office. Try her there."

23

MR. ALGER SHOVELED a large morsel of chocolate cake into his mouth and began to work his jaws with pleasure. He smiled at Vita who was sitting next to him on the sofa and used his dirty fingers to cut off another piece. "Delicious," he said, smacking his lips. He pushed some crumbs hanging on his chin into his mouth with a smudged forefinger.

Finally he slapped his thighs. "Well, I'm filled up, I guess. I usually don't have too much appetite this time of day because I usually have a sucker in my mouth. Keeps me from getting hungry."

He smiled at Vita and squeezed her thigh. "Let's go into the bedroom, Vita."

"Won't you have some more cake, Mr. Alger?" she said.

"No, I've had enough for now. I might take a piece with me later."

He tugged at her arm. "Come on, Vita. I want to see you naked."

"The tea's still warm. Wouldn't you like some tea?" she asked trembling.

"No," he said. "Let's go into the bedroom." He tugged at her arm, not quite as gently as before. She rose from the sofa and let him lead her into the bedroom. He closed the door and pointed to the bed, "Lie down there, Vita," he said. He pushed her gently toward the bed and pressed her down with his hand. She fought an almost uncontrollable urge to scream. She knew someone would hear her, but his strong hands might throttle her windpipe before they could help her. I mustn't let myself panic, she thought. He killed those women because they panicked and screamed or fought back. Or because he was frightened and knew he had to strangle them. She lay still on the bed waiting for his next move.

"Let me take this off," Mr. Alger said. "You'd better sit up." She sat up obediently and he lifted the pink slip over her head.

The sight of her white body in nothing but a white brassiere and panties made his eyes gleam. "God, you're pretty," he said. He looked at her and then said almost shyly, "Is it all right if I take off the brassiere and panties?"

She nodded slowly. He turned her over and undid the catch of the brassiere. It fell away from her breasts quickly. Then he tugged at her panties until they came down her long legs.

"God, you're beautiful," he said, "back and front." He turned her reverently and looked at her. He sucked in his breath. "Oh, you're beautiful," he repeated, staring in fascination at the open book that was her body. He bent his head and kissed her breasts, then he cupped them in his hands. He kneaded their firmness with his fingers, while Vita closed her eyes, her temples throbbing so horribly she thought they would burst. When she opened them there was a glazed, animal-like look in his eyes. He squeezed her breasts so hard that it was all she could do to keep from cying out in pain. He stared at her hypnotically and dug his fingernails into her thighs. His eyes worshipped her legs, breasts and face. He was so worked up now, he could not keep from trembling.

"Oh God," she thought, "please don't let him kill me." Her fear of being raped had been supplanted by a terror that he would tear at her flesh in a bestial fury or strangle her in a fit of passion. But he continued to caress her in a gentle way.

His hands moved over her belly and toyed with her navel. He laughed as his finger probed her navel. Then his fingers stroked her thighs. Once his fingers touched the edge of her pubic area and they darted away as if he had touched a flame. He concentrated on her thighs, kneading them with his dirty fingers. Vita shuddered as he dug his nails into her flesh.

"What's the matter?" he asked in a hurt voice. "You said

136

I could play with you. You look nervous. What are you so nervous about?"

"Nothing," she said trembling. "Nothing."

"You're not expecting anyone, are you?" he asked suddenly. "You're not expecting this Palmer fellow or the cops?"

She shook her head, unable to speak.

"Okay," he said. "If I thought you called anyone, I'd have to kill you." He played with her a few minutes longer. Then he sprawled on the bed and hugged her close, pressing his lips against hers. She could breathe in the stale odor of his unwashed body and the rank smell of his clothes. His breath smelled of a mixture of raspberry and peanut butter. He pressed himself against her deftly, digging his fingernails into her back and began to issue odd noises from his throat. She realized with horror what he was doing and a nausea overcame her.

Suddenly they heard the doorbell ring. Mr. Alger held her tightly against him, not moving. The bell rang again a moment later.

"Who's that," he rasped to the naked, trembling girl in his arms.

"I don't know," she said.

"You tipped off the cops to get me," he accused.

"No," Vita said, paralyzed with terror. "No, I swear I didn't."

The bell rang a third time. He moved his strong hands to her throat. She could feel his body tremble against her own.

"No, please. It's not the police. It's probably a neighbor who wants something. Don't be frightened."

She prayed inwardly that whoever was outside would go away. If they tried to force their way in, he would strangle her at once.

There was a silence outside. He lay still with his arms around her throat. "They'll never get me," he said, "they got me once in Indiana, but I got away. That was seven years ago and they'll never do it again. If I thought you tipped them off!"

His hands gripped her throat more tightly.

"No," she said in a choked voice. "I wouldn't."

Suddenly they heard the door being forced.

He began trembling all over, and his hands tightened around her throat.

"Please don't. They'll go away," she begged, hardly able to utter the words.

But he was terrified now, and no longer believed her.

"You tipped them," he screamed. "You tipped them off."

He began to squeeze her throat with his powerful hands. Suddenly there was a sound of glass breaking and immediately afterwards the sound of several shots. Mr. Alger stiffened as the bullets entered his back and then his body slumped over the trembling girl's, his hands still clutching her throat. A second later Vita's body was convulsed horribly and she was sick on the bed. Then she fainted with the dead man's arms around her throat.

The window was raised quickly as Lieutenant Goldberg, Jim Farley and two uniformed police climbed through. Goldberg was still holding the gun that had killed the prowler. He took a quick look at the hands around the girl's neck and groaned.

"Too late. He's strangled her."

"No," Farley yelled, catching a faint movement of the girl's body. "She's alive. Get him away from there."

The uniformed men pulled Alger's corpse from the bed, disengaging his hands from Vita's neck.

Goldberg moved to the other bed in the room, ripped off the quilt and threw it over the naked girl. "Get some water quick or see if she's got any alcohol."

Farley came back a minute later with a bottle of blackberry wine and a glass. Goldberg patted the girl's cheeks gently and then lifted her head. Vita opened her eyes slowly and saw the men. She screamed, "No! No! They'll go away. Don't kill me," she shouted, closing her eyes.

Goldberg held her head against his shoulder. Then, gently he put the glass to the girl's lips. She sipped some of it slowly.

"It's all right, Vita. He's dead. He can't hurt you. He's dead."

She looked at him and slowly recognized him. Goldberg gave her some more wine. She stared at the body of Alger on the floor and shuddered again.

"My God," she said, "I never thought I'd live through it."

Goldberg instructed the police to take Alger's body into the back yard. As they carried him out, she said softly, "I spoke to him every day and never knew. He was going to kill me," she repeated, as if to convince herself.

"Probably would have if I hadn't shot him through the window," Goldberg said. "You can thank that Thomas girl for saving your life. We thought you were out shopping or something. She called and told us you had sounded a little green around the gills when you called Miss Wright and you didn't answer when they called you back. It was easy to figure what had probably happened."

"I was afraid you'd find me dead when you broke in," she said hoarsely. "He had his hands around my windpipe and I couldn't breathe."

"I was afraid of that too," Goldberg said. "I almost held back because of it. But there's no guarantee about people like that. When they go haywire anything might happen. He might have killed you anyway just because you knew who he was."

"I never thought of that," she said. Her throat felt as if it were lined with sandpaper and had been twisted horribly.

"Did he rape you?" Goldberg asked gently.

She shook her head. "What happened was almost as awful." She shuddered, thinking of it.

One of the uniformed policemen came in. "There's a mob outside. They heard the shots and some of them want to see her."

"No," Goldberg said. "This girl's in no condition to see anybody." He bent over the girl. "Shall I call the doctor, Vita? I can get him here in fifteen minutes, using a squad car."

"No," she said hoarsely. "I'll be all right. My throat's killing me, that's all."

Goldberg looked at Farley. "Jim, make her some hot milk and put a couple of tablespoons of butter in it. Not too hot." He smiled at Vita. "That's what my wife gives me when I got a bad throat. Are you sure you don't want the doctor? You look pretty shot to me."

"No, please. All I need is rest." She did not want to go through the hospital routine again, and she wanted to be there when John came. She wanted, above all, to be able to leave with him in the morning.

The doorbell rang suddenly and she jumped. Goldberg frowned as he saw her frightened reflex. "Damn that jerk. I told him to keep people away."

They heard John Palmer's voice a moment later. He was arguing with the uniformed policeman.

"She's my fiancée," he protested.

Goldberg looked at Vita and she nodded. He walked out hurriedly. John was two feet into the living room and carrying the bottle of champagne.

"For Christ sake's, Lieutenant, let me in there. I want to see her," he yelled, pulling away from the officer who held a tight grip on his arm.

139

"Let him go, Joe," Goldberg said.

Goldberg smiled. "Go on in. She's in fine shape to drink champagne. How come you rang the bell this time? What happened to your key? Or didn't you look under the doormat?"

"Let me in there," John begged. Goldberg nodded.

John rushed into the bedroom and kneeled by the bed. Vita's pallor, the red marks of the prowler's fingers on her throat and the coldness of her hands shocked him. He kissed her lips tenderly.

"Oh, my darling. I should never have left you alone," he said guiltily, wanting to cry at the tired, hurt look on her face. "I had a hunch about this. Are you—I mean, did he?"

She shook her head, her eyes watching his quietly.

"You must feel like hell, baby," he said softly, touching the marks on her throat as gently as he could.

She nodded, smiling wanly.

He lifted the champagne bottle with a sheepish grin. "I never was good at timing. I brought this along to celebrate." He put it on the floor. "We'll have you all right in a jiffy, darling. You can rest here for a few days and then we can leave."

"No," she said hoarsely. "I want to leave tomorrow. I want to get out of this place."

"But you need rest," he protested.

"Let's fly. I can rest in Mexico," she said, speaking slowly.

"If that's what you want, darling," he agreed.

"I can't stand staying here. I don't want to see this place or this town again."

Farley came in with the hot buttered milk. She sipped it slowly and smiled at the detective. "It feels wonderful."

A moment later the doorbell rang again and it frightened her so much she spilled half the milk.

"I'm sorry," she said trembling, trying to keep from sobbing. "I hope you can put up with me," she said. "It'll be a long time before I can hear any kind of a bell without jumping."

It was Alice Thomas. The dark-haired girl strode into the room, sat on the bed and took Vita's hands.

"I think we'd better let her get some rest," Goldberg said quickly. "Let's get outside."

When they had left, Alice stroked Vita's hands gently.

"Stay with me tonight, please," Vita said. "I can't stand being here alone. Even if I know he's dead." She shivered. "God. I don't even know if I can stand being in the dark any more."

140

"You'll be all right," Alice said. "I'll stay with you."

"There's another thing," Vita said. "Please help me take a bath. I feel dirty all over. I can't explain. I have to clean myself. And I feel too weak to do it alone."

Alice nodded and helped Vita into a negligee and into the bathroom. "I can't understand it," she said to Alice, as the hot water flowed into the tub. "He was such a kind, good-mannered man. I must have spoken to him a thousand times and he said 'Yes, ma'am. Thank you, ma'am' and acted as shy as a child."

A moment later as she lay back in the tub, she said, "I hate this town, Alice. I hate it."

"You'll get over it," Alice said, soaping her back. "One town's as good as another. Or as bad."

"No," Vita said. "Los Angeles is horrible because these things happen in the sun. Anyway there's no reason to come back. I'll bet they'll be glad to see me go."

Alice grinned as she sponged Vita's neck gently. "If you ask me I think Helen and Claire envy you more than anything else."

"Envy me?" Vita said incredulously.

"Sure, don't you know every woman secretly hopes she'll be raped by a man who can't resist her? Well, they know it could never happen to them; and they'll never forgive you for being so irresistible."

"You've got the craziest sense of humor," Vita said, but she couldn't help laughing.

"I know," Alice said, "that's why I can't hold a man. Men just want girls to laugh at their jokes."

Vita felt much better. There was a quality of astringent briskness about Alice that was as bracing as a dry Martini.

In the living room Lieutenant Goldberg and Sergeant Farley were sampling the champagne. It was a good, dry wine and they took their time. Finally Goldberg rose and put the glass down. "Let's go, Jim. We're going to be up to our asses in reporters in fifteen minutes." He grinned at John. "If I were you, I'd hide. A love angle goes big in this town. It's full of frustrated housewives who want to gobble up all the juicy details and make up for their own crummy marriages." He paused and turned to Farley. "Jim, let's stop at a jeweler's on the way. I've got to pick up something." He turned back to John. "My advice to you is—blow fast. Or that wife of yours may relent. Models and actresses have more vanity than a French hairdresser."

"This one does," John said. "I'll leave in a few minutes."

141

The detectives went in to say good-by to Vita, who lay comfortably in bed, looking much better after her bath. Alice sat at her side. She smiled in a friendly way to Farley who grinned back.

"You're certainly a handy girl to have around," the Irishman said appreciatively. "You think fast."

"Thanks, the same goes for you," Alice said. Vita was amused to see a rare blush suffuse the dark-haired girl's cheeks.

"Good-by, princess," Goldberg said. "Where you going to be? You staying here?"

"Not a chance," John laughed. "We're heading for New York. I've got a business deal there."

"Oh how I envy you," Goldberg said. "Oh I have a message from Buhler for you, Vita. He was really sorry he scared you to death last night. He took a plane home this afternoon. I think he was frightened of his old man more than anything else."

"I feel awful about pointing the finger at him," Vita said.

"Nuts," Goldberg said. "In the state you were in, you could have pointed the finger at Winston Churchill. Or me or Farley. Well, we'd better go."

"Yes," Farley said, not taking his eyes away from Alice. "I've got to get home. I've got some unfinished business there."

"I wish I knew how to thank you both for saving my life," Vita said.

"For what?" Goldberg asked. "It was just in the line of duty. Routine. I'm a servant of the great city of Los Angeles. Coming, Jim?"

"Yes," Farley said. He seemed reluctant to leave. They shook hands with Vita and Farley took Alice's hand. "See. you around maybe," he told her, his Adams apple moving as he spoke.

"I hope so," Alice said quickly. "I'd like to see the police setup sometime," she finished weakly.

"You would?" Farley said grinning. "Sure. I think you'd find it interesting. I could show you the teletypes, the line-up, everything."

"When?" Alice asked.

"Oh, anytime. Just call me anytime you're free. And maybe we can have dinner or something afterwards." Farley looked relieved and in his embarrassment shook hands for the second time with everybody.

"Would tomorrow be all right?" Alice asked persistently. "Around six?"

"Oh sure," Farley said. "It would be a pleasure." He reddened as he saw Goldberg's smile. "I'll expect you."

After they left, Alice sighed. "I'm afraid Emily Post would never approve of my approach. But I've tried every other method and it just doesn't work. This is a tough town for us working girls."

Goldberg and Farley walked through a knot of onlookers and policemen toward their cars. "She's a nice girl, Jim. And she must be able to cook if she's a home economist."

"Yes," Farley said grinning. He stopped at a phone booth. "Let me call home a minute, Abe. I'm worried about Tony."

While Farley phoned, Goldberg stared at the dying sun. It hung over the Hollywood Hills like a great crystal globe filled with blood and its waning strength burnished the peaks of the hills and bounced off the shiny tops of scores of cars moving on streets below them.

Farley came out a few minutes later. "Well, he's not talking much, but at least he's willing to have dinner with me." He looked at the sun. "God, that's a beautiful sunset, isn't it?"

"That's the difference between you and me," Goldberg said thoughtfully, "I don't think it's beautiful. I hate it." He pointed to the tangle of quiet residential streets below them and the figures of some schoolgirls in shorts and skin-tight jeans.

"No, I don't think it's so beautiful," Goldberg said examining the street scene pensively. "Before I came here I felt like Becky did. I read the technicolored ads about Malibu and Hollywood and the palm trees and the ever-loving sun. After being here four years and clocking some of the sex crimes that go on in the Goddamned California sunshine, I'm not so worked up about it anymore. Too many nuts come to this town: firebugs, sex bugs, cheap crooks, religious fakes, and assorted other shifts."

"I guess in Brooklyn they don't commit crimes," Farley said picking up his cue as he usually did on these debates.

"They don't rape teen-age girls in the middle of the afternoon," Goldberg said so resentfully that Farley was astonished. "You don't find peepers and stranglers in every alley. You ever read the file on sex crimes in this town? It's good bedtime reading—try it. Sometimes I think that God tipped over the United States and let all the queers and creeps slide down to the West Coast. And don't hand me any crap about that sun. To me it's blood-colored and for a damned good reason."

143

"What's all the sour grapes for, Abe?" Farley said good-naturedly. "We got the prowler, didn't we? We saved the girl."

"We got *him*. But how many more? And how about that poor kid who got her neck twisted like a chicken in the alley the other morning? I'm sick of this town. There's death stalking the streets. It's been poisoned for me. I think I'm going to resign and go back to New York where they have honest-to-God racketeering and burglary."

"Baloney," Farley said grinning. "You're just unhappy because we didn't take the prowler alive. The publicity would have made you a captain. But you'll get it anyway and you know damned well Becky isn't going to move back to New York."

Goldberg shrugged. He took a last look at the sunset as it reddened the roofs of Beverly Hills and the distant sky over the invisible Pacific Ocean. "Just don't ever expect me to like this town. I can't. Come to sunny California, they tell you in the ads!" he said acidly.

He gave the beautiful sunset a long, loud, sincere Bronx cheer and opened the door of the car.

THE END